WINSTON'S AMAZING WORLD

Dawn Davis

FIRST PRINTING, July 2020.
Harry Markos, Director.

Paperback: ISBN 978-1-913359-84-3
eBook: ISBN 978-1-913359-85-0

Book design by: Ian Sharman
Cover by: Ramon Salas
Editor: Darren G. Davis

www.markosia.com

First Edition

PROLOGUE

In the dimension of Atzil three children appeared seemingly from nowhere. There was a four-year old boy and a pair of fifteen-month old twins, a girl and a boy. The older boy was mute and the other two were too young to speak. Their clothes were tattered and dirty. The older child clutched the girl in his arms while the younger boy held on to the eldest's shirt. Their parents could not be found and no one knew them.

The two younger children were sent to live with a wealthy widow who was cold, self-indulgent and arrogant. As they grew up, they became like her.

A shepherd took in the older boy and taught him to see the good in all people and the beauty in things, which were considered ugly. He was a compassionate man who had very little, but was extremely generous with what he had. The boy understood everything but did not speak. Being a very simple man, the shepherd did not know the child's name and not wanting to call him by the wrong name, affectionately called him Boy.

The children were allowed to visit with each other once a month.

Boy would go to the marketplace with the shepherd to trade for supplies. There he noticed a beautiful young girl with raven black hair dressed in a pale green smock. She smiled at him and he shyly responded in kind.

One day when Boy was about sixteen, the girl approached him at the marketplace. The gaze of her emerald green eyes in his was mesmerizing. "My name is Suri, what's your name?" she finally asked the boy, who had not uttered a word in the last twelve years.

He stood there for a moment, lost in her eyes, "Shadel," he said in a puzzled whisper.

Later that evening when asked by the shepherd why he was suddenly able to speak, he had no answer. He questioned Shadel about his past but the boy truly had no memory before that first day and he knew only what the shepherd had taught him.

When Shadel and Suri were not helping out with their families they loved the idea of being able to help others in need. Suri would tend to a sick mother who was unable to care for herself or her children. Shadel would help an injured farmer. Together they would bring food to those who did not have.

Suri was a great storyteller; children would gather in the meadow to listen to her stories. The young friends never seemed to sleep; they were always out assisting others.

Shadel continued through the years to have his monthly visits with his brother and sister. The younger siblings were always well dressed and ill-mannered while their compassionate older brother dressed as a simple shepherd. He dearly loved the twins and wished he could spend more time with them.

When they had free time Shadel and Suri were inseparable and would meet, spending endless hours talking together. They dreamt of creating a perfect world although it seemed so farfetched. Together they agreed in their perfect world there would be challenges for the people to overcome so they could appreciate what they have and what they have accomplished.

Seventeen years after Shadel arrived in the dimension of Atzil, it was late one afternoon as he tended the flock in the distant field when he came upon an apparition of an ancient man. Startled by and in disbelief at this sight he asked, "Who and what are you?"

"I am Atika, a spirit sent to you by the benevolent ever-present energy force. The time has come Shadel for your destiny to be revealed. You are to be the one to create a cosmos. In doing so, you will become an omnipotent immortal and rule as King.

You will become one with the ever-present energy force. This will happen when you reach the age of forty. Speak of this to no one. I will visit you each night to prepare you for this event. The girl called Suri is to be your queen. She too will become immortal as will your brother Avadon and sister Angeen since they are of your blood."

CHAPTER ONE

As he walked along the path next to the stream, Winston listened to the serene sounds of its gently flowing water. He was on the path that led to the hiking trails and lower caves of Mount Rellon. Before his father, Simon, left five years ago on a mysterious mission for King Shadel, the two would spend hours hiking in the mountains and exploring its caves. It was here in these familiar surroundings Winston could almost feel his father's presence.

It was a clear warm day. A soft breeze blew through the leaves of the trees that grew near the banks of the stream. Despite today being the anniversary of the day his father left on that mission and the fact he had just celebrated another birthday without him, twelve-year-old Winston was determined to make this a pleasant outing. He was going to remember all the good times they spent together.

He watched as dozens of exquisitely colored birds gracefully flew about the sky while a chorus of green and yellow striped birds sang from the trees. A kaleidoscope of butterflies nourished themselves on the fragrant flowers growing along the path. Winston was feeling at peace in this tranquil setting when someone lightly brushed against him. Turning quickly, he saw nothing. "Humm!" he thought, "What was that? My imagination must be working overtime," he reasoned.

Not giving the incident a second thought, he continued walking when he began to notice the birds and the butterflies were all gone. In fact, aside from the sound of the flowing water there was silence. "That's a little strange," he said aloud but still not paying much attention to what seemed to be happening.

By the time Winston neared the hiking trail, his mind turned to the night his father left. He can still clearly see himself that fateful evening sitting next to his father on their rooftop balcony. The glistening stars filled the clear night sky. Closing his eyes, he could visualize his father turning to him and gently saying, "You know I have to leave in the morning for a time, my sweet son. King Shadel is sending me on a very special mission. The details of this mission must absolutely be kept secret. All I'm able to tell you is, there are people far away who are in extremely difficult circumstances. A long time ago these people were tricked and taken a great distance from their homes. They're very unhappy and in a lot of pain. They need to come home but they don't know how. My mission for the King is to help these people prepare so they'll be able to return home. Now Winston, the King has made it possible for me to visit with you in your dreams while you sleep. I'm told it will seem as if I'm really there." At seven years old that simple explanation satisfied him. He felt proud of his father for being chosen by King Shadel, the Ancient One.

Occasionally during some of his dream visits when he endeavored to get more information from his father regarding the mission, all Simon would gently say was, "Winston, I know how hard this must be to accept, but I've told you everything I'm allowed to reveal. I wish I could tell you more but I can't. You know I wouldn't be away this long if this mission wasn't crucial. People's lives are at risk. My sweet son, I promise you, you'll understand everything one day. However, for the present, I need you to trust me."

"What I don't understand is where could my father be that he can't at least come home for a visit? It would take a little over a day's travel from the farthest continent on Luminatia to our home in Manadir."

He missed his father terribly. Particularly now, given that for the first time his team has made it to the semi-finals of the Ring of

Splendor Race. This was huge in his young life! The race is a major annual event on Luminatia, with people traveling great distances just to watch and he was going to be part of it! Winston longed for his father to be there even though he knew it was impossible.

After twenty minutes or so of hiking upwards on the trail and deep in thought, Winston heard an earsplitting horrific echoing bang and then another. Startled, he turned back looking towards the stream which a short while ago had appeared so tranquil. That tranquil stream now resembled a raging ocean. Waves were violently smashing against its banks. The sky darkened and powerful winds seemed to come at him from every direction.

"What in the world's going on?" he shouted aloud. "This is so weird. I've never seen or heard of anything like this ever happening anyplace on Luminatia," he nervously thought as he instinctually headed towards the caves to find cover.

As he ran for shelter, the winds blew so fiercely that he was knocked off his feet several times. Winston tried holding on to whatever he could find to keep himself upright. He tried ducking between some large boulders along the trail for protection. It was no use; the winds ripped him away. Loud sounds of howling began to fill the air. The entrance to one of the caves was now in sight. He gathered all of his strength and made a dash for it.

Once inside Winston collapsed against the cave wall. Bruised and shaking profusely, he had never experienced anything like this. "What's happening?" he yelled. Fear permeated through his entire being as the howling took on an eerie unworldly quality. "Maybe I'll be safer at the back of the cave," he thought.

He took out the small torchlight he always carried with him, lit it and slowly began to move further into the cave. Once more he felt something brush by him. Turning quickly again there was nothing. The howling turned to high a pitched shrieking.

Dark shadowy forms appeared and began taunting Winston. "Who are you? What are you and what do you want from me?" the young boy screamed, his body trembling. There was no answer. "Oh, what's that smell?" he cringed, looking around to find the source of the putrid stench which was now filling his nostrils. He saw nothing.

Winston was under attack; by what or who he had no idea. These shadowy black figures were coming at him from every direction. There were hundreds of them. They had no particular shape as they brushed by him emitting a slight stinging sensation, which sent chills down his spine. Terrified and screaming, "Get away! Get away!" Winston began swatting at these shadows with his arms.

"Winston, Winston," his sister Willow called out. "Wake up! Wake up!" You're having a bad dream.

"Huh! I was dreaming? Wow! It felt so real," he said sitting up and still trembling.

"Winston you never have bad dreams. Are you ok?" she asked concerned about her brother.

"Yeah I'm good," he said sounding a little disoriented. "This is gonna sound crazy, but it feels like it was a warning of some kind," he said rubbing his eyes and beginning to relax.

"A warning!" his sister repeated feeling a little uneasy. "A warning about what?

"I don't know, I can't remember anything about the dream now. I just have this feeling, I can't explain it," he replied.

"You must have eaten one too many cookies last night. Winston you've got a real vivid imagination." Willow chuckled.

"Speaking of eating, I'm starving, I need some breakfast."

"You're always starving," Willow said with a smile as the two headed down to the kitchen.

CHAPTER TWO

Willow watched from the rooftop balcony of their townhouse as her older brother, older by eleven minutes practiced for the Ring of Splendor Race. Winston sat atop Bracer as they soared across the clear blue sky appearing to head directly into the sun. But then they made a rapid turn into a severe dive, an abrupt twist, and a backward loop. Next it was straight down towards the ground and another quick turn across the horizon. She studied her brother as he practiced in earnest.

Seeing malgrids fly so gracefully in the sky always fascinated Willow. As Bracer, Winston's white dove bodied malgrid with its golden beak glided above her, she could see the purple, green and gold markings on its white transparent butterfly shaped wings. Malgrid's wings were deceiving. Giving the impression they were ever so delicate, when in fact they were powerful enough to break a large branch off a tree with one flap of their wing. She had seen malgrids fly while carrying the weight of heavy men on their backs with such seeming ease.

Like all children in the idyllic world of Luminatia, on the day the twins turned five, their young malgrids flew into their lives. No one is sure how the malgrids know when appear into a child's life, but it is always on their exact fifth birthday. It is one of the mysteries of the ages. Because a child is able to communicate with their malgrid telepathically, some people think there might be a psychokinetic connection that ignites once a child reaches the age of five.

Others are more philosophical and believe in the legend of Vidad. He is the young hero from ancient tales who is purported to have discovered the species of malgrids, also known as aeropaths, on a remote island and tamed the first one. When his younger brother Morlen saw Vidad flying on the malgrid he yearned to fly with him. Vidad's love for his brother was so great he tamed a second malgrid and presented it to Morlen on his fifth birthday. A powerful lifelong bond was formed between the aeropath and the young boy. From that day forward legend says when a child on Luminatia turns five a malgrid arrives specifically for that child and they immediately bond for life.

As Willow continued to watch her brother perform some of the difficult maneuvers, she wondered how they could share the same DNA. Although they were twins, they were not identical. Both had light brown hair and hazel eyes but the similarities stopped there. She was serious in nature; Winston on the other hand was a bit of a jokester who loved making up stories for their adventure games. Willow was slender and petite with long wavy hair, while Winston, about two inches taller than his twin was slightly on the stocky side, but not fat, kept his hair short. She loved art and music. Winston could not be less interested in either. If it did not involve an adventure or solving a mystery, if it could not be taken apart, examined, explored, reconstructed or flown across the sky, to her brother it was not worth knowing or doing.

After an intense practice session, before landing, Winston decided to take a quieting flight on Bracer to unwind. As he flew over his home in the City of Manadir, the capital and largest of the cities in Luminatia, Winston began to take deep breaths releasing the remnants of his pent-up energy from his long practice session.

He guided Bracer, flying low as they passed over the white limestone tri-level home he shared with his family on the outskirts of the city overlooking Lake Mornea. Winston knew concentrating his attention on these tranquil sights always helped him to relax.

Focusing on Manadir he caught sight of the copper dome of the Royal Museum of Natural History where his father, Simon, had been the assistant curator. He smiled remembering the many times he had accompanied his father to the museum when it was closed and the adventures they created together in the many exhibits. Those adventures still sparked his imagination.

Bracer flew him high above verdant Great Forest with its stately evergreens. Even at this height, their fragrant scent tickled Winston's nostrils. At the forest's edge, Winston caught a glimpse of the Ancient One's castle overlooking the Shevac Sea.

Continuing to concentrate on the visions below he felt the tension in his body begin to leave. Fusions of color framed the gardens breaking up the vastness of the monochromatic lawns as the sunlight danced off the golden doors of the majestic white marble castle. North, at the far end of the castle grounds he spotted the Royal Aquarium with its unique and colorful underwater life forms. From above, he could make out the carvings of fish on the three bluish-green marble columns at the entrance to the white stone building housing the aquarium.

And then he saw it, the grassy field where the semi-finals and finals of the Ring of Splendor Races are held each year. This was the year he would be racing in that field. His heart seemed to skip a beat. It was located only two thousand yards west of the castle itself. Within the next two weeks that field would be transformed into a stadium.

In the past he had been only a spectator at the event. He had been awed by the young racers' flying proficiencies and their abilities to memorize and execute the intricate sequences needed to accurately fly through mazes of brightly colored rings.

Winston smiled as he remembered the first time his father took him to see the Race when he was six. He sat next to Simon in the bleachers bewildered, and yet fascinated by the sight of these spectacular rings. They were like perfect circles of fireworks, bursting into the air as if by magic in an assortment of brilliant colors, sizes, and positions.

Winston delighted at the possibility of flying through those rings one day. Closing his eyes, he would imagine what it would be like guiding Bracer with great speed and precision through the actual rings as the crowd cheered. Now he was about to find out. His long hard hours of practice were hopefully going to pay off. The feeling of excitement sometimes felt overwhelming as he realized he was about to live his dream in what was an important annual event in Luminatia.

It has been said the children of Luminatia, to honor King Shadel and Queen Suri on their wedding day created the Ring of Splendor Race thousands of centuries ago as a tribute. The magnificent spectacle symbolized the magical rings of light worn by the king and queen.

It was working. As he concentrated on the wondrous sites of the city he loved, all the tension and stress of his practice session had disappeared.

Winston and Bracer glided over the city with its pristine white limestone structures and well-manicured parks then headed inland towards the Surruhe Mountains. That was probably his favorite place. The mountains were breathtaking and inviting. He dreamt of someday climbing them and exploring the hidden caves. Thinking about caves, Winston's mind jumped back to the previous week when he, his best friend Godfrey, Willow and Pru, Godfrey's younger sister, had gone down into the caves under Godfrey's house pretending to be pirates. As pirates they spent the afternoon looking for buried treasure while fending off an assortment of imaginary creatures and black-hearted pirates. They always saw themselves as the good pirates, who would find treasures and help the less fortunate. Playing the part of a pirate was Godfrey's favorite game.

As Winston guided Bracer towards home they flew over vast hillsides covered with wide blankets of brilliant colored wildflowers. In the distance he saw Lake Mornea and the edge of Great Forest at the far side of the lake. Winston thought of how his mother and sister would love this scene knowing their passion for painting.

He was proud of his mother, Anessa Lane. She was one of the most renowned artists in Luminatia and known for her use of vibrant colors. Her work hangs in some of the most prominent homes and galleries in Luminatia.

Winston knew his twin sister dreamt of following in their mother's footsteps. Even at twelve, Willow was quite the budding artist. But what was his dream? He had no idea. What were his special talents? He thought about it but nothing came to mind. Although he occasionally wondered what his life might be like when he grew up, at twelve he did not seem to have a direction. His mind and body relaxed now and back down on the ground; he ran towards his house.

Winston burst onto the balcony where Willow and his mother were talking. Out of breath he blundered in as if he was in middle of their conversation, "So Godfrey and well…he and Pru want us to come over and go exploring in the caves. Whatta think Will, you up for it?"

"Sounds like fun," his sister answered.

"Go ahead and enjoy yourselves, please be back in time for dinner," Winston and Willow were already out the door and running down the stairs, when their mother shouted her last command. Anessa knew with Willow by his side, Winston would be safe. "He, the captain of reckless adventure; she, the level headed philosopher," she thought smiling.

Their malgrids were waiting for the twins as they rushed out of their house.

A feeling of exhilaration always filled Winston as he observed the mountain vistas from up high. "Bracer, whenever I fly over these mountains ideas pop into my head for some awesome adventure stories. Everyone says I've got a great imagination. Hmm! I wonder…is that my talent making up adventure stories? But then what am I supposed to do with that? Become a writer?" He thought about it for a few seconds. "No, no, that can't be it. That's a really dumb idea," he groaned attempting to contemplate his options for his future. First of all, I don't like writing and besides I'm not very good at it anyway. Telling good stories is one thing writing them is another. There's gotta be something else. I just don't have a clue what that something else is," Winston said aloud.

"Are you talking to Bracer again? Willow quipped.

"Yep! He's a good listener," he said joking with his sister. Then with a serious tone in his voice Winston turned to his twin as she flew next to him on her malgrid, "Will, you know what you'd like to do when you're older."

"Of course, be an artist like Mother," she responded.

"Well that's the thing, I've been thinking lately, our friends have all kinds of potential and they're really good at stuff. For instance, Godfrey, he's a great athlete. He's good enough to be a sports star someday? Or maybe even a statesman, he's smart, very diplomatic and he's a born leader. Then there's Pru, she's smart, funny, and thoughtful. She likes discovering things. Maybe she'll be an archeologist like her father. And of course, you're going to be an artist like Mother. Then there's me! It doesn't look like I have any talents that could lead to anything," he said perplexed.

"If you can't find any talents now, maybe it's just because they haven't shown up yet," she said encouragingly. "What do you think you'd like to do?" she asked.

"What I really want to do seems kinda unrealistic, like having adventures. I sometimes think about where I might find new places, what's out there to be discovered? I like adventure, mystery, things that are unusual with maybe a little danger thrown in for fun," he quipped.

"You like danger, Winston this is me you're talking to," Willow teased. "You're the one who always likes to play it safe. The only risks you're comfortable with are in pretend adventure games."

"Well maybe the idea of danger, not the real thing," he said smiling back at her. "The problem is the stuff I like to do, like exploring or adventure, people do for fun, it's more like a hobby. Not for their life's work."

"I guess," she replied. "Winston, look at it this way, you're twelve and your future is a long way off. Who knows, there could be something unexpected that comes up and you'll discover you have new amazing hidden talents," she said trying to be supportive of her brother.

"You're right Will, I'm getting a head of myself. At my age I'm sure nothing life changing is going to be happening to me anytime soon. I'm obsessing for no reason. There are lots of years ahead of me to figure what I'm supposed to do with my life," he nodded to his sister. "Besides, we're here. I can see Godfrey and Pru. By the way, thanks for being a great sister."

CHAPTER THREE

Godfrey and his younger adopted sister, Prunella, otherwise known as Pru waited for their friends on the grounds of their home in the countryside near the university. Godfrey, a tall, muscular, boy of twelve with shoulder length, dark blonde hair hurled the valessphere in the air, trying to master yet another game. He threw the round weighted sphere straight up. No matter how hard he tried to control it, the sphere would land several yards from where he was standing. "I hope we get to be pirates today," he thought to himself as he waited for his friends. Godfrey considered the idea of swashbucklers the epitome of adventurous games. Finding buried treasures, swinging on a rope across the bow of a ship, sword fighting, it all intrigued him.

Pru twiddled with her long French braided raven hair entwined with lavender ribbons and wondered what part she would get to play in their adventure game today. Her green eyes were filled with excitement as she scanned the distant horizon awaiting a glimpse of the malgrids that would carry their two friends here for an afternoon of fun. She loved the fact that even though she was about a little over a year young than the other three, they always included her in their activities. The reason they liked having her around Willow once told her, was because she was funny, thoughtful, precocious, fearless and probably wiser than the lot of them.

Pru liked Willow and thought she was sweet, very pretty but kind of girly unlike herself who she deemed to be more like one of the boys. Except for the ribbons she always wore in her hair.

She took the burled wood and brass spyglass from her pocket, a gift she received for her eleventh birthday. Although the gift was from Winston and Willow, Pru preferred to think it was Winston's idea to give her what she considered to be such a unique and spectacular gift. As far back as she could remember, Winston has always been her favorite of all of Godfrey's friends, but since her party Winston was looking a little different to her. Butterflies seemed to flutter in her stomach. She could not quite grasp the cause. But it usually happened when Winston was around and her heart sometimes began beating a little faster.

Pru always had a great sense of humor and was never at a loss to quickly think of something funny to say. Nowadays her brain seemed to go numb when he was around. She liked being considered one of the boys. Competing with them to see who could climb higher or run faster. Though lately something else definitely seemed to be going on inside of her. "Maybe it was the new responsibilities she was given not long ago," she reasoned. "It couldn't be Winston. No! He's just my buddy," she groaned to herself feeling slightly befuddled over the possibilities. "Who would have the answer?" she wondered. "I couldn't ask Mama. No, absolutely not, she would tease me and want to know, 'When is my little rough and tumbler going to become a young lady?' Willow's the young lady, not me," she thought.

Gweneen, her adoptive mother, taught ancient history at the university and took pleasure in the rugged lifestyle digging in the dirt and camping out at remote archeological sites with her husband, Jonathan, an archeology professor. Occasionally they would bring Godfrey and Pru with them to the sites. She enjoyed seeing and sharing with her children what she referred to as ancient history coming alive at these digs. While her mother was an attractive, petite woman with beautiful long red wavy hair, she was most comfortable in jeans and a t-shirt. Pru did not consider her mother as particularly lady like. She saw her as a grown-up type of rough and tumbler and could not understand why her mother seemed to want her to become a young lady?

She wondered if her teacher, Staishya, a Butterflian Shapeshifter, would have the answer. "Yeah, she might know about butterflies fluttering around in my stomach, after all she's a butterfly who changes into a woman." These thoughts quickly left her mind as she spotted two tiny specks in the distance flying towards them. "I think I can see them," she said to Godfrey handing him the spyglass and pointing to the sky.

They watched, as the specks grew larger until they were able to make out the shapes of the two malgrids. As they landed, Pru, feeling a little awkward about her recent thoughts, ran directly to Willow, trying to pay as much attention to her as possible while attempting not to focus on Winston.

"What's the adventure going to be today?" Winston asked polling the group for suggestions.

"What about being archeologists looking for a new civilization?" Willow replied as the four friends headed down the long winding path leading to an extensive series of caves and tunnels which ran beneath Godfrey and Pru's house and the nearby university.

Jonathan would often remind his son, daughter and their friends that some of the tunnels in these caves have been deemed safe for them to play in, but others are considered dangerous. He told them, "Rock slides have been reported in some of the deeper recesses of the caves. One tunnel was found to have a foul smelling, toxic bubbling substance erupting from some cracks on the floor." Knowing that both children and adults would explore the tunnels, the university sent in a crew of geologists to clearly mark the areas safe and unsafe for entering. As an extra precaution, Jonathan, periodically would walk the youngsters through the tunnels making sure they all understood which areas were safe and which areas they were forbidden to enter. Everyone has to adhere to the rules. Especially Pru, who he always describes as his little fearless rough and tumbler, mixed with a bit of a daredevil because she was constantly looking for something to climb up, to jump off of or run to.

Jonathan took great pleasure in stimulating young minds. Godfrey and Pru were never aware that while they were at school their father, would occasionally go down into the caves where they played. He would salt parts of the tunnels with lots of brightly colored stones, beads, fake gold coins and replica of various artifacts he either found or purchased, for them to find. His children and their friends knew their finds had no real value but were always delighted with their endless discoveries.

"What about pirates? We could be pirates and hunt for treasure." Pru chimed in. "What do you think, Winston?" she asked. She looked at Winston waiting for a response to her suggestion about a pirate game. "He's cute," she thought, "Ick! What am I thinking?"

Knowing pirates was Godfrey's favorite Winston smiled and asked Pru, "What kind of bribe did Godfrey give you to suggest pirates?"

"Can't tell you, it's a secret," she teased.

"We just did pirates just last week, what about going to the mystical land of…hmm…of Trope," Winston suggested as his imagination thrust into full gear creating fictitious names, places and a scenario for their make believe adventure, "to retrieve the sword of Har and save the world from the Accus. We'd have to cross the land of the boiling mud and go through the caves of the Invisibles. I heard there are some nasty creatures living in that mud. It's gonna be a dangerous mission, are we up for it?" he laughed.

"Sounds like a good one," Godfrey said punching Winston lightly on his upper arm and nodding to the rest of the group. "We've got a sword to find, let's get moving," he shouted as they all moved faster down the path towards the caves.

Later that afternoon after saving the world the four friends lazily sat on the grass at back of the house drinking lemonade while waiting for the malgrids return.

"They're here," Pru, pointed to the sky as they all got up and walked towards the side lawn to await the landing of two aeropaths.

CHAPTER FOUR

It had been a long day and Winston was tired. He opened the window in his bedroom; the cool night air helped him to sleep. The rays of the full moon flooded his room. As he crept into bed pulling the covers up over him, all he could think about as he drifted off was having a good night's sleep so he would be energized for practice tomorrow.

At three a.m. the hall clock began to chime, bong, bong and stopped. The shadows of the swaying tree branches outside Winston's bedroom window were suddenly still. Tiny dust partials, which had swirled in the moonlight now hung motionless in midair. Nothing moved in Winston's room, in his house; nothing moved on all of Luminatia. Crickets chirping a second ago were silent as was the owl hooting in the distance. All the sounds of the night had stopped. Time had stopped.

As the young boy lay still in his bed, tiny twinkling lights began to whirl about in the now stationary sky. It appeared at first as if the stars were moving in slow circles, but they were not stars. The stars above had materialized as frozen dots of stagnant light in the darkness. More and more of the twinkling lights filled the vast night sky and covered all of Luminatia. A myriad of twinkling lights entered through Winston's bedroom window and floated to his bed. Gently lifting him up out of the bed, the lights whisked Winston, still sleeping, off to a mountaintop where the boy was carefully set down upon a large rock.

"Winston, wake up, it's Father," Simon said in a very soothing voice as he tapped his son's arm.

"Huh! What?" the boy said startled as he opened his eyes and saw his father sitting next to him. "Father it's you, you're really here," he exclaimed as he touched Simon's shoulder, "this isn't a dream visit is it? Where are we and, and how did

I get here? Father, what's happening and what's this all about?" feeling apprehensive and confused, he rattled off his questions.

"Everything's fine son," Simon reassured him. "It's just a little different and you're right, it's not a dream visit," he said trying to put Winston at ease.

"What are all these twinkling lights? And why are you wearing your bathrobe?" he asked as he looked at his father in a long purple robe. "And you're really here, aren't you?" he continued to question and definitely unsure of what he was experiencing. This was so beyond anything he could have ever imagined; he just needed more reassurance this was all actually happening.

"Yes, I'm really here," he said overjoyed, as he was able to hug his son for the first time in five years.

"Oh Father, I've missed you," Winston said elated, hugging his father as tears welled up in the corners of his eyes. At the same time feeling bewildered by the sights around him. "But what's going on?"

"Be patient my son and I'll explain. Some of what I'm going to tell you may sound very strange at first, but know it's all good and you're safe," Simon said continuing to reassure Winston.

"O…Ok!" Winston stuttered, still gazing around at what seemed like millions of tiny lights surrounding them. "But Father, what are those lights?" he persisted.

"They're beings from the Kingdom of Lights," Simon replied.

Stunned by the perplexing answer Winston's eyes widened in surprise as he stuttered, "Those little lights are beings! From where?"

"The Kingdom of Lights is where the essence of the good people of Luminatia go when their time in this world is finished," his father explained.

"You mean like heaven?" the young boy asked mystified.

"Yeah! Simon smiled at his son's reaction. "Winston, I'm going to touch on the beginning of an extraordinary true story now and understand that very soon the whole story will be revealed to you.

A very long time ago a difficult and complicated situation arose. Ten people very close to King Shadel, the Ancient One chose to form a secret order called the Order of the Light for the purpose of serving the King and the people of Luminatia. Because their service was freely given, he enabled the ten to become guardians and bestowed them with special powers. Since King Shadel is immortal and the ten guardians were mortal, they all pledged that one child, to be chosen by the King, in each future generation of their descendants, would continue the legacy to become a guardian and enter the Order of the Light." Simon leaned in towards his son and took his hand, "Winston, I'm a guardian and the descendent of one of those original ten guardians."

"What? Huh! You're a what?" was about all Winston could get out of his mouth. It sounded too bizarre to be real.

"I know this is difficult for you to grasp. It was for me when my father told me he was a guardian," Simon explained, knowing his son could not possibly understand the implications of what else was to be revealed. "What's happening to you now is called the Dream of Guardians. It occurs just before becoming a guardian. Several days prior to learning their destiny, that person has a terrifying dream. When they awake, memory of the contents of dream is gone. Its purpose is to begin to prepare their consciousness for the transition. Winston, my son, you're about to become a guardian. It is your destiny."

Dumbfounded and not quite able to process all he was hearing, he began to ramble on, "Father, I had a dream like that a couple of nights ago. You mean I'm going to become a guardian...for real? Me!" he exclaimed pointing to himself. "With powers...what kind of powers? What about Willow is she going to become a guardian, is Mother a guardian? What does Mother think of you being a guardian?"

"Slow down son," Simon grinned. "Yes, you will become a guardian and yes in time you will receive powers." Simon's tone turned serious, "No, Willow and Mother are not guardians nor will they become one. Winston, do you trust me?"

"Yes, Father of course I trust you," Winston answered not knowing what to make of the unfolding state of affairs and feeling utterly flustered.

"This must be kept a secret, just between you and me. You cannot tell anyone about this including your sister or your mother. You'll understand the reason in time. I'm going to touch your forehead and you will fall back to sleep and be returned to your bed. When you wake up in the morning you won't remember any of what happened until the day after you've completed the Dream of Guardians," Simon instructed.

"Tomorrow night you'll be brought back to me and I'll introduce you someone very special. For now, my son, know I love you and you're quite safe," Simon told Winston as he put his hand on his son's forehead and the boy fell into a deep sleep. "By the way son," he chuckled as he whispered in Winston's ear while the boy slept, "this is not my bathrobe."

The same twinkling lights that brought him to his father now returned him to his bed. Bong, the clock struck three, the dust once again floated about in the light of the full moon, the shadows of the tree branches outside of his window danced across his room. The crickets chirped, the owl continued to hoot, the noises of the night were back. Time returned.

CHAPTER FIVE

"You'll feel better after a good night's sleep," Anessa reassured her son as she sat on the edge of his bed that night, trying not to show her concern. He had complained about being very tired all day, which was odd for him, he was always so energetic he never seemed to tire. She would keep a close eye on him she thought as she tucked him in and kissed him on the forehead.

Sleep came quick to Winston that night. He did not like to admit it but it was nice to have his mother tuck him even though he thought he was too grown up for that, it still felt good.

The dance of the moonlit dust and tree shadows appeared in his room once again as a concert of night sounds played outside his window. "Bong! Bong!" chimed the clock at three a.m. and then nothing but immobility and silence filled Winston's room and all of Luminatia. Yet again time stopped no motion, no sound, just a heavy scent of stillness.

The twinkling lights returned filling the sky as they had the night before. Once more they entered Winston's room and transported him back to the mountain where Simon waited for his son.

Simon nudged his sleeping son. As he awoke his father asked, "How did it go yesterday?"

"Father, it was weird. I was so tired, I'm never that tired during the day. What's happening to me?" Winston asked with some concern.

"A part of your subconscious mind is being awakened during the process of the Dream of Guardians which is causing your energy to expand and that's making you feel tired. It's a good thing, Winston and nothing to be afraid of. It's just going to take a little time for you to adjust to what's happening. The fatigue lasts only a few days," Simon reassured his son. "It's actually a positive sign, it means you're ready for the experience. The same thing happened to me when I was ready for my journey."

"A journey?" he quizzed his father trying to imagine the possibilities that could enfold in this unexpected real-life adventure. He was about to find out that nothing in his wildest imagination could have prepared him for how his life was about to change.

"Yes, a journey of the best kind! Along the way you're going to meet some unusual and incredible beings." Simon smiled knowing his son could not begin to comprehend what was about to occur nor appreciate all he was about to learn. He was eighteen years old when his father, Yuval had this very same conversation with him right here on this mountain. It took weeks until he was able to process all parts of the picture that was unfolding before him. Why had he been chosen instead of one of his two older brothers? Eventually he realized it had nothing to do with the order you were born into a family or your age. Only the Ancient One, King Shadel knew whom and at what age guardian was ready to enter the Order of the Light.

Still having a difficult time grasping the scope of what his father was telling him, Winston began to feel excited. "Boy, was this an adventure and to think I was just worried about having a dull life," he chuckled to himself, "my imaginary adventures could never measure up to this."

"Winston, I'd like you to meet someone," Simon said as his son looked around confused because no one was there. One of the spheres of twinkling lights came close to where Simon sat with his son. It began spinning, rotating faster and faster until it lost its spherical shape, hovering as only a blur. Sparks of light burst from the sphere, resembling exploding fireworks in the sky. Continuing to spin the sphere grew in size, until it was a little taller than Winston's own height. As it slowed, the young boy was able make out the outline of a woman, surrounded by a glowing translucent light. A beautiful woman with long blonde hair, the most exquisite lavender eyes and wearing the same purple robe as his father, appeared next to Simon. "Son, I'd like you to meet Myadora."

"Hello Winston," she said warmly as she walked over and sat down next to him.

"Uh hmm!" was all he managed to eke out sheepishly, astounded by the extraordinary sight he had just witnessed. "I've never seen anyone change from a little twinkling light into a kind of person," he said gulping while trying unsuccessfully, to appear nonchalant about Myadora's magical appearance. "I, I've seen see my teacher, Staishya when she flies to class as a butterfly and then turns into a woman. She's a Butterflian Shapeshifter you know." Winston stuttered, "But I've never seen..." he trailed off feeling awkward.

She smiled at him, "Your father told you about the original ten chosen to serve the King. I'm one of those ten. Winston, I'm your ancestor."

"I don't understand," he hesitated, "how could that be, you look so young? Don't you need to be very old to be an ancestor? We're talking centuries, right?" he began rambling in total confusion. "I mean you should be in heaven, shouldn't you?"

"I come from a place much like what you call heaven," she said smiling at the bewildered young boy seated next to her, "it's called the Kingdom of Lights."

"Yes, Father told me," Winston offered.

"There are those of us in the Kingdom of Lights that possess the ability to move across time and space for the purpose of assisting other guardians. We have special powers. You'll learn more about that later, but first I'm going to tell you a story. It's something that happened a long time ago and why the Order of the Light was created. Would you like to hear the story now, Winston?" she asked her young descendent.

"Yes, very much so," he declared with great enthusiasm.

CHAPTER SIX

"More than many thousands of centuries ago the time had come for a cosmos to be created. The benevolent ever-present energy force became one with Shadel who was destined to be the entity to perform that task and reign as its omnipotent King. He was loving and possessed the purity it would take to rule," Myadora began to weave her story.

"Shadel took Suri for his queen, they were very much in love. Desiring peace and happiness for their kingdom, together they ruled with love, respect, generosity and kindness. In turn they were beloved by all their subjects."

As she spoke, Winston was able view the story as her very words formed a rich tapestry of images right before his eyes. "Was this magic? How's this possible?" he marveled in confusion at what he was witnessing. "I feel like I'm there while it's happening, but I'm still here."

There in front of him was a stunning green-eyed slender woman carrying two baskets filled with beautifully colored roses. The vision appeared so genuine he thought he could reach out and touch her, but hesitated. If he dared would her image wash away like a ripple in a pool of water. The woman's waist length black hair tied back with a blue ribbon brushed against her flowing blue dress as she walked out of the rose garden towards the awaiting carriage drawn by four white horses. "I can smell the roses in the garden," Winston exclaimed finding it difficult to believe his senses, "I can feel the heat of the sun but its nighttime here."

"Who is she? Can she see us too?" he asked Myadora nattering in amazement and without giving her a chance to answer. "It all looks so real," he persisted.

Myadora smiled, amused by Winston's bewilderment over the scene. "They're shades of the past. They cannot see nor hear you and you cannot touch them." She took Winston's hand and guided it towards one of the phantom rose bushes. Their hands passed through it without causing any disturbance.

"Winston, some guardians like myself possess the ability to create visions where one can see, hear, smell and experience the environment, sense emotions and thoughts but they have no bearing in this world. They are simply reflections of what has been," she replied to the wide-eyed boy. "That woman is Queen Suri. She is where we shall begin our experience today."

"Staishya told us about the Queen in ancient history class," he spouted as he continued to watch the vision, which seemed to disappear whenever Myadora stopped telling the story.

When Queen Suri spoke, it surprised Winston. It was not at all how he imagined a queen's voice might sound. She sounded more like his mother, than his perception of royalty. She was not loud or snooty, harsh or brash. Her voice was light and soft as velvet.

"We're going to visit the school on Covered Street today, Finney," she told to the driver of her carriage handing the thin, balding man in a teal uniform two baskets of flowers for the teachers. "Did you bring the box of sweets for the children?"

"Yes, Ma'am," he replied to the Queen as he helped her into the carriage. "Have some good stories to read to the children today?

"Certainly do," she smiled warmly as she watched Finney take his place at the front of the carriage. Leaving the castle grounds, they rode through the city passing pristine white stone houses, some revealing exquisite beveled glass windows. Exteriors of the houses were decorated with an abundance of bountiful flowering bushes and beautiful sculptured gardens. Continuing along the route there were many houses displaying windows of magnificent designs in colored glass."

The streets were filled with people walking about and visiting shops. Queen Suri smiled and waved to them as her carriage passed by. She was much beloved by everyone and they eagerly returned her wave and smiled back at their queen.

Myadora turned to Winston; "She knew everyone in the kingdom by name and occasionally would have Finney stop the carriage to talk with some of her subjects. Wishing them a happy birthday if appropriate or acknowledging some other occasion. The Queen was always very thoughtful and caring."

The scene he had watched vanished from his sight in a puff and was replaced by the Queen reading to a group of children.

As she was finishing the third story for the younger children, a teacher for the older children interrupted, "The children are ready for you on the boquent court."

"Thank you Merrilina, I'll be there momentarily," Queen Suri replied as she handed out sweets to the young children and invited them to watch her play boquent tag with the older children.

Winston watched as the Queen and three children paired up into two teams. Hundreds boquent flies of various colors, with tiny oval wings, flew around in the enclosed court.

Holding her soft open racquet first in her left hand and then shifting it to her right hand Suri passed a purple boquent fly through the hoop, then went for two flies, three flies and when she finally was able to get four flies to pass through racquet at the same time she scored. Then she turned and tagged her partner, a stout dark-haired boy on the shoulder who then took his turn. There was cheering as players scored. One of the flies got tangled in the curly red hair of a young player, her partner a thin short boy ran to her rescue. He carefully released the unharmed fly from the young girl's hair. Children on both teams giggled with delight to be playing one of their favorite games with their Queen.

"Wow it's hard to believe she's a queen, she acts like such a regular person," Winston commented.

In the blink of an eye the scene changed. Far off in the distance was a figure of an elegant dressed man in a purple jacket, white pants and black boots. He was riding a sable horse on what seemed to be a road in the countryside. As the rider came closer, Winston noticed his shoulder length blonde hair and his full beard. "Wait, stop!" Winston abruptly interrupted. The vision instantaneously froze, resembling a luminous three-dimensional colored photograph. Staring in awe at the sight before him, "That looks like The Ancient One." Winston stressed in absolute wonderment, "It *is* The Ancient One, but, but he looks the same as he does now, Myadora how's that possible?"

"Yes Winston, it is King Shadel," she replied as she took the young boy's trembling hand in hers. "The Ancient One is immortal. Part of being immortal is the physical appearance doesn't change," she said calming the boy as the vision continued.

Shadel noticed a farmer with his clothes, hands and face covered in mud standing in the field next to a plow. The ox pulling the plow was stuck in a ditch. The king rode towards farmer. "Are you having trouble with your ox, William?" Shadel asked the farmer who looked startled by his visitor.

"Yes, Sir," the farmer replied, "my ox stumbled into the muddy ditch as I was plowing the field. He seems to be stuck and I haven't been able to get him out."

"Perhaps if the two of us try," Shadel said as he dismounted his horse and removed his jacket. "We'll put a rope around the ox's middle and attached it to my horse. He'll pull as you and I push the animal from the rear."

"But Sir, the mud," the farmer said baffled by the thought of his King getting dirty on his account.

"Come on William, a little mud never hurt anyone," Shadel replied as he jumped into the mud filled ditch. The King sunk into the mud completely covering his black leather boots and part of

his white trousers. "There's a lot of fields to plow so let's get this ox out of here," he said as William now joined him in the mud. The two began to push on the ox's rear as the King's horse tugged at the front. The ox grunted. As they continued pushing, they both kept slipping down into mud. It took the two men a short time to free the ox. Climbing out of the ditch, the King looked at William and began to laugh at the sight of his companion covered completely in mud.

William looked down at his mud-covered body and then at the King, who was a sight. He put his hand up to his mouth, "Oh my! Sir, umm, your clothes! Your hair! Your beard!" The farmer stood frozen gazing at his mud-covered King laughing and not knowing what to do.

"It's ok William," the King said still laughing as he walked over to the farmer and put his arm around the bewildered man's shoulder. Both men were now laughing.

Winston captivated by the phenomenon he was experiencing, watched the vision change. He now observed a tall, thin man with black hair and a long straight nose seated at a dining room table. Next to him was a woman wearing a gaudy red dress, her black hair piled high atop her head. At the head of the table were Shadel and Suri. As the King lifted his glass to make a toast, Winston inquired, "Who are those other two?"

"That's the King's younger brother and sister, Avadon and Angeen, they're twins," Myadora answered giving her eager young audience a brief overview of what was coming up. "The King loves them. Unlike Shadel and Suri, the people only tolerated his younger siblings in the kingdom because of their relationship to their rulers. Unfortunately, they were not pleasant. They were arrogant, egotistical and treated people with contempt. There was one wish they knew the King would never grant them. That was to rule the kingdom. Avadon and

Angeen were jealous of the way the people adored Shadel and Suri and wanted that adoration for themselves."

The scene changed and Winston watched Avadon and Angeen walking down a wide path in the forest that led to a clearing.

"When I am king AND, someday, I will be king," Avadon *touted confidently, as he conveyed his habitual arrogant attitude to his twin, "things in Luminatia will change. I will be a powerful king unlike my brother who is weak. He only wants love and peace for his people,"* he mocked. *"Well, as their new king these people will obey my every command or there will be consequences."*

"And when I'm queen, they will all see how beautiful I am, the women will envy me," his sister sneered as she pulled a small looking glass from her purse, admiring her image. *"The men in the kingdom will beg for my attention. But how is this going to happen? Our brother will never step down."*

"By magic, my sister, by magic!" he snickered. *"There's book hidden somewhere in the tunnels beneath the castle called "Secrets of Dark and Evil". It's a book of spells! Magic spells! Our brother hid this book long ago because he claimed he didn't want evil in the kingdom. I'm sure in reality he wanted make certain no one could be as powerful as he. Besides a bit of evil will be good for the people, it might be interesting to see them squirm,"* Avadon said *sarcastically. And then with great certainty he began to spout, "I will find the book and when I do…"* he trailed off in thought.

"Where is he now and what is he doing?" Winston asked as he saw Avadon tossing debris.

"He's beneath the castle in the tunnels. For centuries Avadon has spent most of his time down there in a relentless search for the book. The dimly lit tunnels are a maze filled with many doorways some leading to rooms, to hidden passages and some leading nowhere," Myadora answered as they watched Avadon stealthily prowl about the tunnels.

Winston looked on as Avadon approached a small wooden door covered by centuries of dust and cobwebs at the end of one of the tunnels.

Pulling away the cobwebs he began coughing from the dust. Catching his breath, he attempted to open the door. It was stuck it would not budge. On his knees he tried pushing against the small door with his shoulder several times until his shoulder ached…nothing.

"This door is going to open," Avadon barked angrily. Because the door was low, he laid down on his back for leverage, his feet slightly elevated, determined he endeavored to kick in the door. After numerous tries it finally gave way and opened into a small musty room filled with old boxes. Avadon made such a racket in trying to open the door, he was sure someone must have heard him. Now standing upright he began checking the tunnel to make sure he was safe. Bending to enter the musty room he began pulling away boxes when he spotted a crack with a small hole in a wall. He tried to peer through the small hole. It was dark on the other side.

Winston sat on the edge of his seat cringing at the sight of Avadon's excited expression.

"Hmm!" Avadon sounded as his eyes widened. He removed a small torch from his belt, lit it and tried to squeeze his hand holding the torch through the hole. The light from the torch revealed another room on the other side of the wall filled with more boxes and debris and no apparent entrance other than the tiny hole, which was much too small for him to climb through. He removed a small pick ax he had hidden under his shirt and began attacking the hole. After several hours he decided it might be large enough for him to climb through. He struggled; his wiry body barely fit. Once on the other side he found another crack and a room just like the one he had left, he searched and found an even smaller hole, which he attacked again with his pick ax only

to find a similar room. This continued for three more holes with three more rooms.

Exhausted and looking tattered from his ordeal, Avadon was determined; he continued pulling trunks away from the wall. He stopped at once, staring at an iron door behind the trunks. The door was rusted and would not budge as he tried to open it. He tugged, and pulled and prided, nothing, all the while mumbling under his breath. He searched around until he found an iron fitting from one of the trunks. Using it, he was able to pry the door open. Inside the vault piled high on shelves were old papers, books and more boxes, which he feverishly tossed about. Then he noticed one of the bricks in the wall of the vault did not look quite right. Using the iron fitting he removed the mortar from around the brick. Anxiously, with his hands shaking he reached in. Breathless, his heart felt as though it was exploding in his chest as perspiration ran from his forehead, he couldn't stop. "I can feel a book, it's a book," he shouted as he pulled the volume out of its hiding place. "It has to be the book" he insisted with his eyes closed, afraid to open them for fear of disappointment. Slowly he opened his eyes and gazed at the dusty tattered book in his hands. The title read, "SECRETS OF DARK AND EVIL". "Shadel, my brother you're finished," he said clenching his teeth. His body, aching, scraped, bruised and dirty, trembled. It no longer felt real; he was running on pure adrenalin.

Winston winced at Avadon's reaction.

Squeezing once again through the holes in the walls he ran panting towards a room in the tunnel near the exit where he had hidden some clean clothes. This was something he always did when he went sneaking around the dusty and dirty tunnels. He slid the book into his leather shoulder bag.

Once inside the castle, filled with frenzied anticipation, he raced down the right corridor to his sister's apartment. He pounded on the oak doors. "Angeen, Angeen," he shouted as he hammered the door with his fists.

The door opened and, in the doorway, stood a woman all rumbled in nightclothes with curling ribbons in her hair, some which were beginning to become untied. "What are you shouting about?" Angeen said rubbing her eyes, "it's the middle of the night. You'd better have a good reason for waking me."

"You silly cow," her brother replied as he pushed past her entering the large ornately furnished living room, "Let me in quickly. I've got it," he announced to his sister as he pulled the book from his leather shoulder bag.

"You've got what?" Angeen asked still yawning and seeming totally indifferent to her brother's excitement.

"Fool, focus, get the cobwebs out of your tiny brain," he ordered. "The book with the magic spells, potions and incantations. The forbidden book, that's what I found. Shadel and Suri will be history, I'm going to rule Luminatia," he triumphantly declared, then realizing he would need Angeen's help he amended his statement, "We're going to rule Luminatia."

Queen Angeen, I like the way that sounds," she said rising up off the large red sofa where she had been seated and standing next to her brother staring into the looking glass as she tried to fix one of her curl ribbons which was falling out of her hair.

"What Avadon didn't know, is that the book of "Secrets of Dark and Evil" had been written in codes and parts of it was in an ancient language, foreign to Avadon," Myadora explained as Winston was transfixed to the vision before him. "It took him years of pouring over the book until he believed he was able to decipher a potion which contained a spell to facilitate what he and his sister wanted; control of the kingdom. During that time, he hardly left his apartment."

"Angeen," Avadon called as he banged on the door of his sister's apartment late one evening. "I've done it! I've finally done it!" he

spouted sanctimoniously as he entered and flung himself down on
the sofa leaning his head back against the gaudy red velvet cushion.

"Done what?" she replied with her arms crossed, standing in
front of him. "You mean you've deciphered the book," she gasped
as if a light went on in her head.

"That's right, I've decoded the spell and the recipe for the
potion. Here," he said elated as he handed her a piece of parchment
containing the ingredients for the potion. "Tomorrow I leave for
a very remote area in the eastern part of the kingdom. If I go in
disguise no one will notice me and I will be able to easily use the
spell I've deciphered on our brother's subjects. It will be with great
pleasure to see how they turn against Shadel and follow me. Then
they will adhere to my every command."

"You, my dear sister, need to collect the ingredients for this
potion. When I return you will prepare it and make certain our
beloved brother and sister-in-law drink it. It will transform them
into pathetic babbling imbeciles and their beloved people will
turn from them in disgust," he prophesized. "The spells that I'll
cast will make the people worship and follow us."

The visualization stopped; the large rocks of the mountain
hidden by the vision were once again visible. "What happened?"
Winston asked eagerly, puzzled by the abrupt halt of the images.

"I can only tell you what happened next," Myadora explained to
her impatient descendent. "It would be too dangerous for you at this
time if you were to witness Avadon casting this spell. The powers
you will be receiving as a guardian have not yet been bestowed upon
you. In a short time when you begin to receive those powers then
and only then will you start to understand how to keep yourself
safe. Don't concern yourself now, there's much for you to learn," she
reassured him as she continued telling him the story.

"The next day, as promised, Avadon left for the outskirts of
the eastern part of the kingdom. Once there, he encountered

two men walking down a quiet street. There was no one else in sight. Avadon, disguised as a frail old man, walked over to these men and began reciting the incantation. Mesmerizing both men with the spell, as they stood motionless. Avadon created veils or layers of illusions in their minds making them completely forget the wonderful memories of their lives in Luminatia. In their place, he then created new negative memories of misery and hardship. What was unknown to Avadon was a side effect of the spell he was casting. It was twisting him into pure evil. Vapors of positive energy left his victims' bodies and flowed into his. As the vapors entered into his body, the positive energy was then transformed into hatred and depravity. The book had fooled him by letting him believe the codes he deciphered would turn him into a beloved king like his brother, in fact it had the opposite effect.

The vision returned as Winston saw Shadel seated at his desk, in what appeared to be an office. Sitting on the other side of the, desk were two somber faced men clad in dark green ornate uniforms.

"Sir!" the man with the red moustache began in a grave tenor, "we've had extremely alarming reports from the east." Dalgranca one of Shadel's emissaries continued, "I'm afraid, Sir, your brother is causing severe devastation to the people of that region. Chaos has erupted and many thousands of people are missing."

Calmly Shadel asked, "Do we know exactly what he is doing to cause chaos?"

"Sir! Witnesses have reported he has been gathering small groups of people together, he then delivers an incantation to them," Veon, his trusted aid reported to the King with great concern. These witnesses claim to have seen a white vapor emanating from each of those people and that vapor then turned black as it flowed into Avadon. Your brother has also been altering their physical *appearance so no one can identify them. In some cases, there have been reports of physical violence breaking out amongst the people."*

Shadel stood, "Gentlemen, thank you for bringing this to my attention. I'll look into this and deal with it immediately."

Winston watched as a messenger delivered a small wrapped box to Angeen's apartment that same morning. Inside the box is a parchment folded in four.

Opening the parchment, she read the message:

"Dearest Sister...I think it would be quite thoughtful of you to prepare a special beverage for our beloved brother and his wife today. I'll be returning very soon... Your Loving Brother, Avadon."

After discarding the parchment into the lit fireplace, Angeen understood Avadon's message and rushed into her bedroom. Eager to prepare the potion she sat at her dressing table snatching various ingredients she had previously concealed in bottles of perfumes and lotions and put them into a crystal decanter.

"The Queen's favorite nectar," she uttered aloud, grinning, as she reached into the cupboard for the bottle containing the fragrant nectar she believed would mask the vile taste of the potion's ingredients. "When they drink this their minds fail and they will become idiots who can only babble nonsense. They will become nasty and will be hated," she rambled in a childish contemptuous glee.

Later that morning Angeen brought the gift she had prepared of nectar in a crystal decanter to Suri. "I've prepared something very special. It's a delicious, sweet nectar just for you and my beloved brother," she exclaimed ever so sweetly. "I hope you'll enjoy it with your lunch today, my dear sister-in-law. It contains the nectar of the rare pristol fruit that you love so much," she gushed.

"Angeen, how thoughtful, of course we'll have it with lunch this afternoon," she said kissing her sister-in-law on the cheek.

"Just before lunch the queen opened the decanter and detected a peculiar odor coming from inside the bottle. Not wanting to hurt the feelings of her sister-in-law, she emptied the contents from the crystal decanter into a ceramic jar and refilled it with her own nectar," Myadora added.

The nectar in the ceramic jar began to steam. "That's very odd," Suri thought as she observed the jar break apart. Feeling uneasy she summoned the great sage, Zachonier, to her chambers.

As she described the circumstances he said with great apprehension, "My Queen, Avadon and Angeen wish to harm you and Shadel. This potion comes from the book, Secrets of Dark and Evil. I fear somehow Avadon discovered this book. Many years ago, the King knowing the chaos it could cause hid this ancient evil book in order keep Luminatia safe. Without this book there can be no evil. One needs to have very specific insight to interpret and reveal the secrets of this book. In the wrong hands, whomever attempts to use this book will turn evil," he cautioned the Queen.

"Is the King aware of this?" she asked.

"Yes"

"Thank you Zachonier," she sighed. "I'm meeting the King in the garden for lunch." Suri picked up the crystal decanter filled with her own nectar and walked down the corridor to the garden.

The scene was of the king and queen in the garden. "Winston, tell me what you see?" his beautiful ancestor inquired.

"It looks like the King and Queen are having lunch in the garden," the young boy responded.

"Yes, look closely at the bushes," Myadora directed.

"Oh, it's Angeen. She's hiding in back of the hydrangea bushes," Winston pointed to the barely visible woman crouched down behind two large bushes.

"She can see Shadel and Suri but she's too far to hear what they are saying," said Myadora.

"Your own brother and sister, Shadel, what will you do?" Suri asked.

"I've always overlooked their silliness, their greed, their arrogance. They're my brother and sister and I love them," he replied distraught.

"I understand," she consoled him.

"He's returning to the castle tonight and I'll deal with him then. He's become an extreme danger to the people of Luminatia. He must be stopped. Suri, I fear there could be a real possibility that I may have to put him to death. I don't want have to kill my own brother. He's immortal and you know I'm the only one that can remove his immortality," he agonized. "As long as he has that book there's going to be a potential danger to everyone," he said sadly.

"What about the alternatives to imprison or banish him. I know how difficult this is for you, Shadel," she said with great sympathy as she poured her husband a glass of nectar unaware they were being observed.

"Those are alternatives, but they may not be harsh enough to protect our people," he responded. "I will speak with him later and hopefully get him to agree to banishment."

"They drank it, they drank it!" Angeen giddily sang to herself as she watched Shadel and Suri drink what she believed to be her gift. Carefully, she left her hiding place unnoticed and hurried back to her apartment to await her brother's return.

CHAPTER SEVEN

That night unaware he had been found out, Avadon walked swiftly down the corridor to his apartment. As he opened the door, he noticed the shadow of a man seated in the large baroque chair by the fireplace. Startled, he shouted, "Who's there?"

As the room lit up, Shadel stood up and turned around, "It's your brother."

"Why are you in my apartment?" Avadon asked nervously as he cowered in front of his brother, then noticed Zachonier standing in the corner. His demeanor was quick to change. He stood straight holding his head up high.

"Secrets of Dark and Evil," Shadel announced glaring at his brother. "I want it back now," the King insisted.

"Well that's not going to happen," Avadon smirked. "It's gone, this time and I've hidden it," he shouted contemptuously as a chilling smile came across his face. "You know the power of the book belongs to the one who has possession and I have possession. You would have to locate it to regain possession. It's in a place where you'll never find it," he bellowed feeling all-powerful.

"You may have acquired some power, my brother, but remember, I am the King! I have the ultimate power," Shadel avowed staring into his brother's glazed eyes.

"The penalty for using spells and potions from the Secrets of Dark and Evil is death, Avadon," Zachonier proclaimed moving from the corner of the room to face the younger sibling. Avadon's mouth fell open.

"You wouldn't, you couldn't kill me," Avadon shouted in defiance, knowing Shadel was the only one with the power to change an immortal into a mortal.

"I will give you three options to choose from my brother. Be put to death, imprisonment for eternity or banishment. The same goes for our sister," Shadel vehemently declared. "The choice is yours."

"Knowing he had already hidden many thousands of people who were under his spell in a world of Egoshen, Avadon agreed to banishment," Myadora revealed to her young companion who sat spellbound by the story unfolding before him.

"Does King Shadel, I mean did King Shadel know where his brother took these people." Winston queried not having the patience to wait for the answer "Did he? Uh!"

Laughing at his enthusiasm Myadora responded, "Yes Winston he knew."

She continued. "King Shadel traveled to the other world and removed the veils of illusions from the minds of all the people. He explained to them what his brother had done and why and the choices he gave Avadon. The people understood if they were to return to Luminatia, Avadon would no longer have a kingdom to rule.

They realized as long as he was still in possession of the book 'Secrets of Dark and Evil,' Avadon would find ways to return to Luminatia and persist in generating havoc. Shadel could never allow that and eventually would have no choice but to put his brother and sister to death. The Luminations knew having to execute his siblings even to protect his people; the King would be tormented by that act for eternity. Their love for their King was so unwavering they would not allow Shadel to be put that position.

The people were aware despite what he had done the King still loved his brother and sister. They knew as long as Avadon believed he had a kingdom to rule, he would leave the rest of the people in Luminatia alone. Those who were taken asked the King to return the veils of illusions to their minds. Shadel was so overwhelmed by these people and their sacrifice he vowed to find a way for them to return home.

Allowing Avadon to believe he had the upper hand, Shadel agreed to have his brother and Angeen banished to Egoshen. Avadon would be allowed to retain and rule over the people he had taken. But the younger sibling wanted more. Avadon wanted a bigger kingdom.

Shadel further authorized only three of his brother's representatives from Egoshen would be allowed to come once a month, two hours before dawn on the day of the new moon. They were permitted to take anyone found on the streets during those two hours back to Egoshen. Avadon in return agreed if any of the people brought to Egoshen were able to lift the veils of illusions from their minds without Shadel directly removing it for them, they would be permitted to return to Luminatia.

When Avadon consented to all the terms of the agreement he made with Shadel, he was convinced that *his* subjects would never be able to get their true memories back without Shadel's direct interference. After all he believed he was now omnipotent and invincible. Therefore, in his mind anyone who he wanted to remain in Egoshen would never return to Luminatia.

Avadon's error was in deluding himself into imagining he was so almighty it would be impossible under any circumstances for those he had taken from Luminatia to break any of his spells on their own. Feeling confident of his power over *his* people, Avadon agreed to Shadel's terms. Shadel categorically cautioned Avadon, were he to break any of these rules, no matter how difficult it would be for him, the King would remove their immortality and immediately put his brother and sister to death."

"I know we have a strict law where no one is allowed on the streets at that time, but why did the King agree to let Avadon take more people from Luminatia? He should have said no to that," Winston said adamantly.

"He had his reasons," she said. "The only people who purposefully go out into the streets at the restricted times, are guardians or beings from the Kingdom of Lights who are sent by the King to go Egoshen to help the people learn what they needed to know in order transform themselves and remove their veils. Very, very rarely do actual residents of Luminatia get kidnapped."

"Those are the people my father has been helping to return to Luminatia," Winston gasped as he realized there was the answer to the mysterious mission.

"Yes," Myadora replied acknowledging Winston's long-awaited epiphany as she continued.

"Let me talk with our sister," Avadon begged. "She needs to agree to come with me."

"You've got one day," the King replied.

In Angeen's apartment a short time later after explaining what had transpired with Shadel, Avadon bellowed in his overconfident manner to his sister. "We're going to kidnapped the Queen and bring her to Egoshen. I'll show Shadel about power."

"Kidnap Suri, that's impossible. I've heard our brother has sent her away from the castle and we leaving tomorrow," Angeen said as she began to pace nervously about.

"Oh, my sister, you have so little faith in your new king, ME!" he declared as he pranced and ranted about the room. "I've placed some of my subjects within the castle walls. Our brother is not as smart as he would have everyone believe. He fears me. I've tricked him into letting me send my representatives back to Luminatia to retrieve more people," he announced with great pride, "and when I do, my moles in the castle will assist in the kidnapping of the Queen. They will bring her to my emissaries who then will transport her to me."

"Does the Ancient One fear Avadon? I thought he was, is fearless, Winston asked Myadora seeming somewhat baffled by Avadon's ranting.

"Not at all," she reassured him. "Remember, Avadon's spell backfired. One of the effects it has on him is he's become delusional. It's what he believes not what's true. Unknown to Avadon, beings from the Kingdom of Lights have been with him and Angeen ever since Shadel ordered their banishment. He's aware of everything they say or do."

Winston observed as the vision introduced a new scene. Shadel and Suri, now noticeably pregnant, were seated on a floral sofa in what appeared to be cozy cottage in the forest. Images of dancing light filled the darkened room lit only by flickering flames of the roaring fire in the fireplace.

Holding Suri's hand, Shadel gazed warmly into her emerald green eyes insisting, "No! You cannot allow yourself to be kidnapped, I absolutely will not hear of it."

"My dearest love, it's the only way to truly protect our people. I'm aware there are beings from the Kingdom of Lights there to help our people, but my energy force is much stronger than theirs. Part of your agreement with your brother is you cannot interfere. Besides you're needed here. It only makes good sense for me to be in Egoshen. My positive energy force will help protect our people by making it easier for them to work on removing their veils of illusion. Without a strong positive energy force around them, Avadon might prevent them all from ever returning home. I don't want to be parted from you my love, but it's the only way," Suri declared ardently as she stood and walked to the window of the cottage looking out at the clear night sky lit up by millions of tiny sparkling stars.

"No, we'll find another way," he whispered to her as he put his hands around her waist bringing her close to him and buried his face into the side of her neck. "And what about our baby?"

"Our baby will be here in a few weeks and I've made arrangements for Beka to take the baby for its own protection

and bring the child to a couple very loyal to us. They will pass the baby off as their own until it's safe. You know no one in the kingdom other Beka and Myadora even knew of my pregnancy, I hid it well. This way our baby will also be safe from Avadon."

"Shadel in his heart new she was right but couldn't bear the thought of being separated from his wife and child," explained Myadora as the vision went forward six months.

"It's time," Suri announced to her trusted friend.

"Myadora, that's you with Queen Suri," Winston proclaimed pointing to the vision of a lavender-eyed, blonde woman standing next to Suri in the rose garden outside the green shuttered, white cottage with the gambrel roof.

"I was and am her devoted friend and confidant," said Myadora.

"Suri, are you sure?" Myadora questioned her friend with great concern in her voice.

"Beings from the Kingdom of Lights who have travelled to Egoshen reported back. Avadon has been creating unspeakable chaos among our people who he has taken and apparently it keeps getting worse. I have to go; I don't have a choice. I need to give my support to the ones that have gone there to help as well as our people who are there. They need to be able to draw on my positive energy force. You understand," she said softly to her worried friend, "I have the power to minimize Avadon's power. If I'm able to reduce some of the pain he's causing, it's essential I go."

"I know you're right," Myadora said sadly at the prospect of her dear friend leaving. "It won't be the same here without you," she sighed. "Shadel, he'll be distressed."

"I believe in his heart he's known all along that I would have to go," she affirmed. "Tomorrow is the new moon. I'll ride my horse into the forest and feign an accident. Avadon's emissaries will find me and believe they've kidnapped me. I'll take Grayson and Marvel with me," Suri told Myadora explaining her plan,

"they always bark at the slightest sound, which means in the forest they'll probably be barking all night long. I'll be assured the emissaries will find me. You and the other's close to Shadel need to be there for him. I'll be back," she avowed.

Grayson in his long black fur coat with a white stripe between his eyes, and Marvel with his shiny black coat lay on the dark forest floor next to Suri who positioned herself on the ground pretending to be unconscious after a fall from her horse. They barked at the owl hooting nearby, at the rustlings of the branches in the trees, at all the sounds in the night announcing to anyone able hear that someone or something was here.

A retched stench rose up Suri's nostrils akin to rotting compost, causing a gag reflex in her throat as she attempted to lay perfectly still for her impending perpetrators. The two barking dogs surrounding their mistress poised to attack and began to growl at the slithering sounds approaching. Three foul smelling lime green creatures appeared out of the forest at the edge of the clearing in plain sight of the two growling dogs.

When their scent detected these huge, foul snake-like monsters, Grayson and Marvel begin to cower as the disturbing opponents stood upright to a height of eighteen feet and a width of three feet. Their heads resembled a dragon with a coiled horn protruding from the center of their foreheads. There was a narrow, curved scorpion tail ending with venomous pincers and skin that oozed slimy, putrid smelling pus.

"What are those things?" Winston gulped and gagged at the sight and stench of the horrific creatures he was witnessing before him in the vision, "and how did they find her?"

"Those are harufanks. They were one of the evil inhabitants living in Egoshen before Avadon arrived and became part of his army. The harufanks are the emissaries sent to Luminatia to kidnap. They possess the ability to hypnotize their subject into believing they are actually someone they know," Myadora responded. "When they come through the secret window which is the entrance between the two worlds, harufanks have a radar like ability. They're able sense anyone in this world who is not in some type of shelter. Instantly they can to transport themselves to that specific location in Luminatia."

Winston's focus returned to the vision.

Peering through her almost closed eyelids, Suri witnessed these creatures stare at her two large animals, hypnotizing them. Grayson and Marvel quieted down now believing that these harufanks were three of Shadel's guards.

Two of these hideous, repulsive smelling harufanks slithered towards Suri, as she lay motionless. As one of the creatures rose up, two extremities similar to arms began to protrude from its snake like body. Hovering over Suri, it bent down and scooped her up. She felt the warm, disgusting ooze dripping down her arms. The creature placed her on the back of the awaiting harufank, as its two extremities emerged holding the captive secure, while the third harufank held the attention of her two dogs.

Believing they had hypnotized their unconscious captive, the three harufanks slithered in the direction of the hidden window, which led to Egoshen, leaving her two sleeping dogs behind.

"Someone needs to tell Shadel," Winston declared frantically, apparently getting caught up in the drama of the vision.

Smiling at him Myadora said, "He knew. Later that morning he called together ten of their most trusted and loyal friends, of which I was one."

Winston continued to watch the vision unfold.

"It pains me to inform you that Suri has allowed herself to be kidnapped by Avadon's emissaries," Shadel told the men and women seated with him around the burled wooden table. "She knew her energy force was needed to support the people in

Egoshen, without it they would never have a chance to return home. Avadon's energy would eventually crush their souls, her presence there will permit her to defuse a portion of his negativity while allowing him to believe he is in total control."

A look of great sadness was visible on their faces, "I believe I speak for all present," said Zachonier resolutely turning his head and looking at all the faces around the table, "we're here to do whatever is necessary to help our Queen in her quest and to make sure she and our people safely return."

All ten nodded in agreement.

"Going up against Avadon will require various special powers which at present you do not possess," Shadel, told those gathered, "My very dear friends, I'm concerned you might not fully realize what you are about to undertake. This commitment may go far beyond your lifetimes. Avadon and Angeen are immortal and the task ahead could be dangerous or difficult at best even with the special powers I am able bestow upon you. There's a need to bring light into darkness. Please take the night to reflect on what I've said and we will meet again in the morning."

Winston's eyes followed the men and women as they returned the next morning and took their seats at the table.

"Sir, I've been asked to speak for all present," Zachonier announced. "Each has contemplated the risks and task at hand and they have unanimously pledged to do whatever is or will become necessary to accomplish this undertaking. Furthermore, each one has decreed that this pledge will be passed on to one of their descendants in every future generation until the objective has been met. It will be up to you, Sir, to choose those descendants. Those present have vowed allegiance to return our Queen and our citizens to Luminatia. They are prepared to take an oath to this effect and form a secret order to accomplish this. As you said yesterday, Sir, there's the need to bring light into darkness. All ten

are in agreement that it would be appropriate to call this order, the Order of the Light."

The vision ended as Shadel bestowed their powers.

"That night we all took an oath and Shadel bestowed each one with divine powers which would be passed down to each future generation and could only be used in the service of the King and Queen.

Feeling mystified, excited and overwhelmed at the same time, Winston blurted out, "Do I have powers? What kind of powers?"

"No, Winston, you don't have powers as yet," she mused at the boy's obvious enthusiasm. "First you will be required to take an oath to become part of the Order of the Light. It will be necessary for you to learn and understand how to use those powers. There are many different powers. Some guardians have more than one, and new powers seem to come to fit the needs of a situation. We'll talk more again."

"It's time for me to leave now and for you to go back to your bed. You won't remember any of what has happened until after you have been inducted into the Order of the Light," she said as she kissed his forehead then stood and began to spin back into a small twinkling ball of light.

"Father did this really happen or am I dreaming," Winston said almost breathlessly.

"Yes, Winston this is really happening. I know it seems overwhelming in the beginning but I promise you, you'll be just fine," Simon whispered as he once again touched his son's forehead sending him back to sleep.

CHAPTER EIGHT

During breakfast the next morning there was a knock at the door. Curious to see who could possibly be calling at that early hour, Willow went to check.

"I'm Mosee. I have an invitation for Master Winston from King Shadel," the decorous man dressed in a navy-blue uniform announced as he tipped his hat in a very formal way to Willow, "Is the young master at home?"

"Yes sir, I'll get him." Willow answered in a very polite manner as she ran to the kitchen to get her brother. "Winston, the King sent someone here with an invitation for you," she said grabbing her brother's hand and pulling him towards the front door.

"Are you Master Winston?" Mosee asked.

"Yes, I'm Winston," he said puzzled as to why the King would send *him* an invitation.

Mosee handed Winston a large gold envelope with the Ancient One's seal on the back. "The King has invited you an event at the castle. Each year teachers from all over Luminatia nominate students, who they feel have achieved something special. As a reward for their achievements, twenty students are selected to spend a day of activities at the castle. This year's activity is the scavenger hunt." Mosee explains to the young boy.

"I don't know what I could have possibly achieved?" he replied, confused as to why he had been chosen. "But, thank you very much Mr. Mosee," Winston said courteously as the messenger turned and walked away.

"Mother! Mother!" Willow shouted as she ran to the kitchen where her mother was clearing the table, her brother arrived two steps behind, "Winston just received an award from King Shadel."

"An award," Anessa declared. "How wonderful, Winston what did you do to earn an award?" she asked as she put her arm around her son's shoulder, hugging him.

"Mother I don't know, Mr. Mosee said I achieved something special," he said holding the unopened invitation in his hand.

"Well open the invitation and see what it says," she instructed him as Willow stood close bursting with excitement.

"You Are Cordially Invited To Attend A Scavenger Hunt At The Castle This Thursday At Twelve Noon," Winston read. "That's tomorrow," he proclaimed.

"I guess you'll have to wait until tomorrow to find out about the mystery of your reward," Anessa said, "but now you need to get ready for school."

CHAPTER NINE

Precisely at noon Bracer landed on the west side of castle grounds. Winston dismounted, and patted his flying partner gently on his leathery crest as he noticed the four boys and two girls who had gathered at the far end of the side lawn. Walking towards them he spotted Trai, his teammate in the Rings of Splendor semi-finals. Unsure about appearing foolish or imprudent by asking Trai about the supposed achievements bringing this group together, he just said, "Hi Trai."

"Winston, yeah, uh hi," acknowledged Trai. "I haven't seen anyone else here I know, just us. That man near the fountain said we've been split up into two groups. The others landed on the east side of the castle. We're all supposed to hook up after the hunt is over. There's the last of our group coming now," Trai said pointing to the girls walking towards them.

A thin, grey haired man lumbered up the path. His frame seemed much too frail to handle the bulky chest he was barely balancing. "If you would all please gather around," shouted the man struggling to carry the huge chest then dropping it on the ground with a dull thud.

"I'm Larkem, your game keeper. I'm to instruct you on what is expected," he continued, looking up and down at each of the children as if inspecting them for flaws. "There are two groups, you are group One. Group Two will begin the hunt on the other side of the castle ground.

"I have a leather pouch for each of you containing twenty-seven sealed envelopes. Some instructions will be quite specific as to the items you are to find. Others will not name the actual object but will only contain clues to what needs to be found. It will be up to you to determine what that particular object is, in some cases directions will be given."

"You are to find as many items as you can in the time allotted. You must open each envelope in their order," Larkem was quite emphatic on this point. "Should you choose to pass locating or are unable to find the item designated in a particular envelope you may skip it, but you forfeit the right to seek the item later."

"If an object cannot be removed and brought back with you, a picture must be taken using the camera provided in your pouch. A large canvas bag will be also furnished for you to keep your findings," Larkem instructed.

"Each item has been given a numerical value depending on the difficulty involved in locating it and each player has a different set of items to be found. There will be two winners. First will be one of the two groups with the highest collective score, the second will be the individual with the highest score. Is everyone clear about the rules so far?" Larkem asked.

A resounding "Yes" was heard from the group.

Larkem handed the pouches and canvas bags to the eager young hunters. "There is a yellow card in your bag which will give you directions as to where you are to begin the hunt. At the sound of the castle chimes, the hunt will officially begin only then may read your first envelop. The hunt will end at the sounding of the second set of chimes. You will then return here to be taken to the Great Hall. There King Shadel will announce the winners."

"Good luck to you all, you may now read your yellow cards," Larkem said.

Winston pulled the yellow card from his pouch and read, "Follow the path beginning where the yellow balloons are tied to a tree, your destination is blue." Looking around he spotted the balloons and followed the path lined with large bushes. "Hmm!" he wondered, "destination blue. What the heck does that mean?" A little further down the path he noticed a small bush with blue flowers. He smiled, satisfied he had located his destination and figured this was going to be easy. He waited there for what seemed like an eternity. Winston was excited to get started. Ten minutes went by before he finally heard the sounds of the castle chimes.

Immediately he pulled the envelope marked number "1" and quickly tore it open. It read, "one cream colored cone shaped shell with brown, orange and gold striped markings."

"This really is going to be easy, there are lots of shells by the sea," he said aloud. Feeling confident he put the open envelope back in the pouch and headed towards the cliffs overlooking the sea at the north side of the castle. The path down to the sea was steep. Wooden steps with railing were built halfway down the cliff. The rest of the way one could easily manage climbing the rocks to the sand below. As he made his way towards the bottom, he saw many different varieties of shells. Walking along the sand Winston scanned the beach for the right shell. "There's one," he shouted as he spotted the cream cone shaped shell. Pleased with himself at his first find, he carefully brushed the shell and placed it in his bag.

"One down and lots to go," Winston announced to the great sea, his arms thrown up in victory. Pulling out and opening envelope number "2" he read, "yellow and black myeeka," "We've got a sea theme going here," he quipped as he tried to recall where he had seen that fish. "The castle's aquarium," he blurted out. "We went on a school trip with our teacher, Staishya I remember she made a special point of showing us the myeeka fishes," he thought as he made his way back up the cliffs towards the path leading to the aquarium.

"This seems too easy," he mused as he reached the aquarium.

As he passed through the columns into the interior of the building, familiar sounds emanated from Winston, "Uuuhhh!

Oooh!" Having visited the aquarium many times he was always awe struck seeing the gigantic tanks filled with what he considered to be the most exotic magnificently colored fish and sea creatures. He delighted at seeing two large, round, purple and orange galenta fish and several white mucans with black spots. There was an elongated magenta colored fish, whose specie he could not remember. The fish appeared to be swimming on top of a white tutu and his favorite a light green sea creature about one foot high that resembled a sea horse.

Fascinated by these remarkable specimens, Winston paused for a few minutes at each tank. He thought how incredible it would be to have the ability to breathe underwater and swim with these amazing sea creatures.

The glass tanks made up the walls, ceilings and floors in all the rooms of the aquarium, creating an illusion of being able to walk through the sea. Different varieties of fish, sea creatures and sea plants inhabited the tanks. They appeared above, below and to the sides. As he entered the sixth room, he spotted it, "Myeeka," he said putting his camera close to the glass as he snapped his picture. "Better take a second, just to be sure," he decided.

Feeling confident at how easy this had been Winston took a few extra minutes to watch the magnificent sea life moving about in the tanks.

Back outside the aquarium the third envelope revealed his next quest, to find a "Dunglun" … point value thirty-five.

Nothing else was written on the card, Winston was stumped, "What's a Dunglun?" he asked aloud. "I've never heard of anything remotely like it," he sat puzzled on the steps outside the aquarium. After a few minutes of wondering he reminded himself, that just a short time ago he thought how easy he believed this scavenger hunt to be. It seems that it suddenly got tough. "It's thirty-five points," he reasoned, "I have no clue where to begin or how to find out what this is. It's probably a good idea not to waste the time and take a pass." Hoping the next challenge would not be as difficult as the last he pulled the fourth envelope.

"Fourth card. Please be something I can find," he said whimsically as he read the card.

"O.O.T.L. Go to the castle, through the left wing locate two doves. Climb thirteen steps, follow the emerald to the golden doors of the hall of lights, locate the crown and there will be the golden chalice."

"Ok! This is more like it. Could be fun, hmmm maybe a mysterious adventure," he mused as he raced towards the castle.

"Hi! I'm Winston, I need to go into the castle, I'm part of the scavenger hunt," he announced to the guard at the entrance to the castle.

"I'm very sorry Winston," the guard in the dark green uniform sternly told the eager young boy. "I have no knowledge of any scavenger hunt and cannot allow you to enter the castle."

"What!" he exclaimed stunned that he could not gain entrance. "But look," he defiantly pushed his fourth card in the guard's face. "It says I have to go to the castle."

"Sorry, young man," the guard said with no sympathy in his voice, "not today."

"B…But!" Winston said pleadingly as the guard ignored him and stared straight ahead.

"This can't be happening," he agonized as he walked away from the castle entrance. "No," he proclaimed aloud, "I've gotta find another way in." He quickly turned and ran towards the side of the castle. When out from behind a clump of tall bushes walked man right in Winston path. The two collided and fell to the ground. "I'm so sorry," Winston said helping the man in the purple robe up. "I wasn't looking where I was going," he said apologetically as he looked at this old man with the sparse waist length curly red hair and scraggily beard which now had a leaf and two twigs stuck in it from the fall. "Sir, are you ok?"

"I'm just fine, young man, where are you going in such a hurry?" asked the man, brushing off his robe.

Winston explained about the scavenger hunt and his plight of not being allowed entrance into the castle.

"Come with me Winston, I'll take you into the castle," said the man.

"How did you know my name?" Winston asked mystified that a stranger would know him. "Do I know you, you look a little familiar, like I've seen you somewhere before?"

"My name is Zachonier, perhaps you've just seen me about," he said smiling with a twinkle in his eyes. "Come with me, I take you into the castle," he said leading the boy back to the castle entrance and right past the guard into the Great Hall. "Have you been in the Great Hall before?" Zachonier quizzed, knowing the answer, just making conversation so the boy might feel more at ease.

"Maybe three or four times," Winston said as gazed at the huge rectangular room with ornately carved golden moldings framing its ceiling, floor and arches. Through the arches were corridors leading to each of the castles three wings. The Hall was enormous. He estimated it could easily hold at least a thousand people. "One time there was a big party here when my mother gave King Shadel a painting she made for him called Malgrids at Sunset," he proudly proclaimed. "Come, I know where it's hung, it's over there," walking across the white marble floor inlaid with a braided gold, purple and emerald green pattern, Winston pointed to a large painting of two malgrids flying over the sea at sunset adorning the wall beneath the great glass dome ceiling in the Hall. "Mother says the King loves art."

"Yes, he enjoys art. The castle halls are filled with works of all the great artisans of Luminatia," declared Zachonier. "Now young man, where is it that you have to go?"

"I have to find two doves in the left wing," Winston replied to his kind companion.

"If you go through that archway there," he said pointing his long, thin finger to one of the gold encrusted arches to the left flanked by two white marble columns, "It will lead you to where you need to go."

"Thanks so much for your help," Winston said as he turned and ran towards the castle's left wing. As he approached, he saw two guards standing just inside the entrance. Fully expecting them to stop him, he hesitated in entering the wing.

"Can I help you?" said the shorter guard.

Showing him the card from the scavenger hunt, Winston gulped and said meekly, "I need to find two doves."

"Go right ahead," the guard replied to Winston's surprise.

CHAPTER TEN

Walking slowly down the corridor, Winston's eyes focus on the many carved moldings, painting and statues lining the hallway as he searched for two doves. Startled by the dark and dreary nature of the paintings and sculptures he encountered, he winced. He was accustomed to artwork with colorful and uplifting subject matter. These works of art depicted different versions of pain, suffering, misery and anger. There were paintings of emaciated people who appeared to be starving, dirty miserable looking children in ragged clothing. One illustration portrayed a man lay bleeding in a filthy rain-soaked street, he had never seen or imagined anything like this. It gave him a sickening feeling in the pit of his stomach. He was beginning to feel extremely apprehensive.

Repulsed by his surroundings it was now vital for those doves to appear quickly, he wanted to be out of there now as he hastened his pace. "Maybe I should just turn around and get out of here. Should I just pass on this card and go to the next one" he agonized as he made his way through the corridor. But something inside of him told him not to retreat, to continue on. He moved more swiftly now, quickly glancing at the paintings, moldings and statues, anxiously trying to locate his next clue. Winston was unaccustomed to this environment. He could feel his palms becoming clammy as he doggedly made his way down the seemingly unending corridor of horrors.

Rushing down the corridor as it veered towards the left, he abruptly stopped. In front of him was a large ornately carved oak door with a golden key shaped handle. His eyes were drawn to the middle of the door. There they were, the two golden doves. Taking a deep breath Winston slowly turned the handle and cautiously began push open heavy door. The eerie screeching sound of hinges rubbing together filled the quiet corridor. He poked his head around the door, and seeing no one, he entered.

Once inside the small oak paneled room, he noticed bookcases filled with books covering three of the walls. In front of the bookcase across from the door he had just entered stood a large desk and chair. At each end of that bookcase there were two more doors. "There must be stairs behind one of those doors," he decided as he slowly opened the first door. "Nope, just an empty room with four blank walls. This one has to be the right room," he said firmly, opening the second door, which was nothing more than an oversized closet.

"Ok," he said feeling perplexed looking around the room at and endless sea of books. "Now how am I supposed to climb thirteen stairs when there are no stairs here?" It was then he saw it, a little yellow book with red printing 'Thirteen Ways to Climb.' "This is just too bazaar," he exclaimed as he took the book off the shelf and opened it. The pages were blank except for first page, which read: 'The fourth door holds the answer.'

"But there is no fourth door," he insisted aloud now feeling frustrated, "this is ridiculous. I think I really want to go home now; this place is really creeping me out."

All of a sudden, hearing what just came out of his mouth, Winston gasped. "This is not right and it's not real," he said taking a deep breath as he sat down in the chair behind the desk. Something felt wrong. He was losing perspective and needed to focus his mind. "I know I'm letting this place get to me," he said attempting to regain the proper assessment of the situation. Realizing what he was now feeling was just the effect of all the negativity of his present surroundings that he had allowed to sneak into his head. The anxiousness and fear were clouding his mind and his judgment. He would not be able to find anything if he continued this way of thinking. All of his life he had been taught about the effects of negativity.

Winston sat quietly for a few minutes. Then with determination and conviction he told himself, "There's a door here somewhere. Just because I don't see it yet doesn't mean it doesn't exist. This is a mystery and I'm gonna solve it, I'm not giving up." Taking another look around the room he returned to the first door. Opening it he went inside the blank walled room. Slowly walking about tapping with his hands, he felt the walls for a clue to a hidden door. In the middle of the second wall his hand brushed across a small bump. Pushing it with his thumb the wall quietly opened into another corridor. There were three odd looking hieroglyphics painted green on a three-foot high wooden door. A feeling of excitement rushed through him as he crouched down and peered inside the small door, which opened into another corridor. Ahead Winston spotted stairs at the end of that corridor.

Carefully, he crawled through the small door, rushing to the stairs. Confounded he remarked, "There are more than thirteen steps here." He stood for a minute looking up at the steps and then decided to climb. "One, two, three, four," he climbed until he reached the thirteenth step. There was nothing there. Thinking perhaps he had miscounted he was about to return to the bottom to start over when he heard a creaking sound. Startled he watched as the stairs above him rose, revealing a white marble archway. Entering the archway, he found a narrow hallway. The walls were covered in white silk and edged with golden carved moldings.

Checking the fourth card again for the next clue, Winston read, "follow the emerald to the golden doors of the hall of lights." "I don't see any emeralds," he though as he made his way down the long hallway noticing the paintings on these walls were even more disturbing than the ones he had encountered earlier. They showed strange looking ominous creatures. The kind he had never seen before, killing men, hurting children. There were depictions of torture, of blood and anguish. His stomach began to knot up. This time he was determined to keep his focus. He told himself these were just paintings of someone's sick imagination but how could someone in Luminatia even imagine these things.

Wanting to get away from these disturbing images, he raced down the hallway almost tripping when he came to a sharp curve to the right. "Emerald," he yelped with delight as he gazed at two columns dividing the hallway. The white silk walls ended. There on the other side of the columns, the walls were covered in emerald green silk. On the walls in the emerald green hallway were gold sconces filled with golden candles. Despair turned to exhilaration.

His heart beat faster as he ran down the hallway. Stopping short, he stood before two large golden doors. Carved into the doors were a series of freeform shapes resembling a puzzle. Each shape contained a large green emerald. Without hesitation, Winston threw open the doors, "Whoa!" he gasped speechless. His eyes widened at the sight of a huge room radiating in a vast sea of flickering candles.

Stepping through the doors, Winston abruptly felt awestruck by this spectacle. The golden room appeared to be endless. As far as his eyes could see, the entire perimeter of the room was lined with rows of white candles in thin golden candlesticks. The candlesticks farthest back against the walls stood tall, about twenty feet in height. Each row in front of the candlesticks were gradually lower. There appeared to be hundreds of rows protruding into the room. Winston mused, "WOW! It must take a massive amount of people to light these candles."

Standing there hypnotized by this display, his mind flashed back to the next clue; "find the crown." Noticing an archway across from the golden doors Winston went through it. He found himself in yet another corridor. "This is like a maze, I go through one, then another one crops up," he laughed.

In this corridor he found three golden doors, one to the left, one to the right and one straight ahead. As Winston moved down the hallway, he decided first to try the door at the end. Tapping his knuckles gently on the door, he heard a deep voice inside the room, "Enter."

Startled and not expecting to hear anyone, he slowly opened the door into a large wood paneled room. There in the room sat two men. The first man sat on a sofa in front of the fireplace, his back towards Winston. The other was in a large winged back chair, his face obscured by the curve of the chair. Something seemed familiar about the man on the sofa who rose and turned to Winston.

"Father," Winston shouted in astonishment.

"Come in Winston," Simon instructed his son as he walked over towards the boy standing frozen to the spot like an animal caught in a strong glaring light.

Visibly shaken, with tears welling up in his eyes Winston blurted, "I don't understand. What's happening? Why are you here? Oh Father, I've missed you," the boy said running into Simon's arms, not giving his father a chance to answer.

With his arms around his son, Simon replied, "Don't worry Winston I promise you it's all good and you'll understand soon. Come over here I want you to meet someone," he said ushering the boy over to the man seated in the chair.

"The crown," blurted Winston, wiping the tears from his eyes. "I'm very sorry Sir," he said recognizing King Shadel in an instant. "I didn't mean, I mean," flabbergasted, Winston babbled, "Sir, I mean, uh, the scavenger hunt."

The tall man with shoulder length blonde hair and well a manicured beard rose up, stood in front of the trembling boy, smiled and said in a gentle voice, "Winston, yes I know about the scavenger hunt. Please come sit with us," gesturing towards the sofa.

Sitting next to his father on the sofa it was then he saw it, the chalice. Placed on the table next to Shadel was a large golden goblet with tiny green emeralds forming the letters O O T L. "Father," he whispered pointing to the goblet. "Find the crown and you'll find the chalice," Winston thought remembering the clue. "That's a chalice, isn't it?" he questioned pointing the goblet.

"Yes," Simon answered.

"Have you tasted wine, before?" Shadel asked Winston.

"Yes, several times at very special occasions Mother and Father would allow Willow and me have a sip of wine. It's very good, but we're not old enough to drink more than a sip," Winston declared.

"I believe this might qualify as a special occasion. I have a delicious, unique wine I'd like you to taste. I'm sure it would be all right with your father if you had just a sip. Does Winston have your permission to taste the wine?" Shadel ask smiling at Simon.

"Of course," he responded.

Shadel picked up the empty goblet as he turned to Winston, "Would you like to go on a little adventure? I understand you like adventures Winston."

"Oh yes!" he said bursting with enthusiasm, thinking how fantastic and totally unbelievable this was. The Ancient One was inviting *him* to go on an adventure.

"Follow me." The King lifted his hand in the direction of the fireplace. The fireplace completely disappeared revealing a passageway. "The castle is filled with secret passages," Shadel said smiling at Winston, motioning for his two guests to follow. Once on the other side of where the fireplace had stood, Shadel again raised his hand at the empty space and a wall materialized.

An indescribable rush of excitement ran through Winston's body. But having his father with him, whom he completely trusted, gave Winston a secure feeling that all he was experiencing, no matter how strange it appeared to him, was ok.

Shadel led Winston and Simon through the passage to another wall. Once again, the Ancient One raised his hand and the wall disappeared. In its place stood two marble columns. They followed Shadel through the columns up three steps to a room with an ornately carved clock hanging over a fireplace. Standing majestically in the center of the room was a large rectangular table surrounded by six high back chairs on each side. A single chair stood at the head. Placed on the table in front of that chair was a crystal decanter filled with red wine.

Shadel walked to the chair at the head of the table and sat down. He motioned to Simon to sit at his left and Winston at his right. Placing the goblet down on the table, he opened the decanter and poured a small amount of wine into the goblet. "It took courage for a boy as young as you to overcome the obstacles and challenges place before you today to get to the chalice of the "Order of the Light," Shadel praised Winston as he picked up the goblet. "By drinking the wine from this Chalice, your memories of the Dreams of Guardians will return to you," he said handing the goblet to Winston.

Bewildered at what Shadel was telling him, he looked to his father for approval before he accepted the Chalice. Simon nodded and Winston took the Chalice from Shadel. Hesitating for a moment, he brought the goblet to his lips and took a long sip of wine. His head felt as if it was spinning. All the memories of the Dreams of Guardians came flooding back into his consciousness. He sat stunned and felt numb for a time attempting to digest all that had happened and all that was happening. Then he turned to his father and smiled, "I remember, Father, I remember the mountain, you, Myadora, the visions. Oh yeah and the purple robe. I guess you weren't wearing a bathrobe," he said smiling and feeling a little embarrassed.

CHAPTER ELEVEN

Bong, Bong, it was a second before three p.m. when the clock over the fireplace stopped. "Sir!" Winston cried out in amazement as he watched the dancing flames in the fireplace become as still as the flames in one of his mother's paintings. "What?" he could not find the words.

"Time has stopped," Shadel, proclaimed very matter of factually.

"Really! How?" Winston insisted astonished at what he was witnessing. "Why?"

"I have the power to stop time, as do some guardians. For the why…today you will, if you consent, take an oath to become a guardian and be inducted into the Order of the Light," Shadel replied.

Still working to comprehend all he was experiencing, Winston turned to his father and asked in all earnest, "Father, can you stop time?

"No, that's not one of my powers," his father answered.

"What powers do you have? Do I have powers, Father?" Winston excitedly queried.

"No, you don't have powers as yet," he said smiling, as he understood his son's insurmountable inquisitiveness, remembering all the endless questions he had for his father when he first became aware that he was to become a guardian. "All your questions will be answered in due time, I know it's hard to be patient when so many new and extraordinary changes are taking place in your life," Simon told his son thinking how odd it felt almost repeating words his father once told him. How odd it must have felt for his father and what would Winston feel when it became his turn to counsel his child.

Shadel led Simon and Winston back to Hall of Lights. Time as Winston knew it had not returned. He stared enthralled at all the motionless flames in the Hall. Two men in blue robes entered the Hall. Winston looked puzzled, "I thought when time stopped everything froze but us."

"Certain people are given the ability to freely move about," Shadel explained as he introduced his two ministers to his guests. "You and your father will be brought to a place where you will prepare for the Order of the Light ceremony which will take place later."

The ministers escorted the pair through a tunnel leading to an entrance. Awaiting them, there was a carriage drawn by three horses. The night air was cool and crisp as they climbed into the carriage. "Father, I'm so confused. It was three o'clock in the afternoon when time stopped, how did it get to be nighttime in such a short time and where are we going?" Winston asked as the carriage headed towards the forest.

"Lots of questions," Simon laughed, "My sweet boy, I know none of this makes sense to you now but simply put, when there's a need for it an illusion of nighttime, it becomes nighttime, when time stops there is no time. As to where we're going, when we get there you tell me."

"That was a curious and weird answer," Winston thought as the carriage drove through the dark forest. Off in the distance he spotted a light. "Is that where we're going?" he asked.

"Yes," Simon smiled.

Moments later the forest path ended and they entered a clearing. "Father, that cottage looks very familiar," Winston, observed as they drove closer. The carriage stopped and the two passengers stepped out, "The cottage!" Winston squealed, "The cottage from the vision. Queen Suri was here."

"The very same one. Let's go inside and get ready," his father urged him.

The white cottage with its green shutters had not changed in centuries. Inside two purple robes hung in the closet waiting to adorn the guardians. "Winston, come sit down, let me explain what will happen at the ceremony. Do you remember when you first met Myadora, how she was light and then transformed into a person?" asked Simon.

"Yeah! It was amazing to see," he answered.

"Well, there will be many more beings like Myadora from the Kingdom of Lights in attendance. It's a sight to behold when they arrive," Simon told his son remembering his first time. "I was in awe, I never imagined anything could be that beautiful, it felt magical." Simon continued, "Just before we leave, your grandfather, Yuval, will join us from the Kingdom of Lights. He will accompany us to the ceremony. Other guardians from Luminatia will there, King Shadel will speak and administer your oath.

An emerald set in a gold medallion will be presented to you by the King," he said pulling his medallion from beneath his shirt and showing it to his son. "Every guardian receives a medallion once they have taken their oath. Each medallion is unique in shape and is a powerful tool. Only guardians have the ability to see the actual medallion to everyone else it appears as a just dull trinket. Carved into the emerald are three hieroglyphics. These hieroglyphics can only be seen and used by the guardian intended for that the medallion. In time you'll learn and understand how it is to be used."

"I'm not sure I can do all of this. I don't know how to be a guardian," Winston sighed, besieged by what he was hearing.

"I promise you, you'll learn in time. I know we all felt like you in the beginning, bewildered and unsure. I understand it seems an overwhelming responsibility, and that's ok." Simon said comforting his son. "But for now, we need to get ready," he said handing Winston his robe.

"Not quite grown up yet, still a boy, but a boy who was about become a guardian It's a lot for his young shoulders to carry, but I know he can do it." Simon thought looking at his nervous young son pacing up and back, playing with his fingers and looking handsome in his purple robe

A tiny ball of light entered the room, "Father," Simon called out as the light rapidly spun, evolving into a man very much resembling Simon. "Winston, this is your grandfather," Simon said as he introduced his father Yuval dressed in a teal robe to his son for the first time.

"Hi!" he said shyly extending his hand towards his grandfather.

"Hi!" Yuval said walking over and kissing his grandson on his forehead. "I've been watching you grow up and you've turned into a very fine young man," he revealed to the wide-eyed boy in the purple robe.

"You have?" exclaimed Winston, "You can see me from the Kingdom of Lights?"

"In a way," his grandfather responded.

"What about Willow, can you see her too?" he inquired.

"Yes, of course, I watch over her as well," he said gently. "It's time for us to leave for the ceremony," his grandfather announced as he took Winston's hand and led him out the door followed closely by Simon to the awaiting coach. A concert of what sounded like wind chimes and blissful music filled the air. It could only be described, as sounds one might imagine would come from angelic voices. "What's that music?" Winston wanted to know.

"It's the choir from the Kingdom of Lights," his grandfather informed him.

"Uuuhhh!" Winston gasped at the sight of thousands upon thousands of twinkling lights swirling around in the night sky.

Simon and Yuval just smiled, knowing that this would be a sight the young boy would remember for all eternity.

As three generations of Lanes climbed aboard the coach, an arc consisting of twinkling lights of beings from the Kingdom of Lights appeared at the foot of the coach forming a roadway across the sky. The lights lifted the coach, floating it effortlessly across the arc to the clearing in the forest set up for the ceremony. As they approached the clearing, Winston looked down, in awe as he saw a huge stone U shaped stadium filled with people in dressed purple and emerald green robes. At the open end of the stadium was a platform. With the coach back on the ground, Yuval led Simon and Winston, who held on tight to his father's hand, towards the platform.

Countless sparkling spheres from the Kingdom of Lights whirled about creating a kaleidoscope of purples, greens, gold and white in the night sky above the stadium. "WOW! Now I get why it had to be night," Winston said breathlessly, almost hypnotized by this incredibly awesome sight. As they approached the platform, Winston could see a golden podium. Several feet to the left but behind the podium were four large ornately carved golden chairs.

Still nervously holding onto his father's hand, Winston followed him up the platform stairs to the chairs. "This is where you'll sit," Yuval directing the boy to the chair closets to the podium.

Waiting for the proceedings to begin, Yuval explained to Winston that the ten men and women, who now stood in front of the platform holding brightly lit candles represented the original ten guardians.

As Winston's eyes followed the line of ten, he gasped, "Pru!"

Trumpets sounded distracting him from Pru. Winston stared at two royal malgrids pulling the royal carriage flying overhead, circling the stadium and landing a short distance from the podium.

The Ancient One emerged from the carriage. A crown incrusted with emeralds and diamonds used only for ceremonies adorned his head. His white silk robe embellished with emeralds and gold piping about the collar and hem blew softly in the breeze as he made his way to the platform.

On the platform he paused in front of Winston, "Are you ready my young friend?" he questioned the nervous boy seated in the oversized chair.

"Y... yes, Sir!" he replied as he watched Shadel walk to the podium.

"My dear friends, we have all come together to bear witness to the induction of Winston Lane into the Order of the Light, so that he may fulfill his part of the legacy," Shadel proclaimed as he addressed Winston, other guardians and beings from the Kingdom of Lights. "As we all know many, many centuries ago people from Luminatia were taken to Egoshen to live in chaos. Queen Suri allowed herself to be kidnapped in order to use her positive energy force to give support to those people.

Luminatia is a land based upon love. Here our people are aware and comprehend the true meaning of happiness. We recognize in Egoshen the people's minds have been fallaciously filled with fear, anger, pain, sadness and uncertainty. The original ten guardians vowed to aid those brought to Egoshen, to help them in transforming their consciousness. First by gaining their confidence and trust and then by teaching these souls how to remove the false the veils of illusions placed in their minds by Avadon. Only then will they once again be able to return to Luminatia, where they will live in an environment of love, kindness and sharing. They have been forced to believe that chaos is the only way they are able to live their lives."

"To achieve this, I have bestowed great wisdom and powers to the original ten and to their descendants upon becoming guardian so they have the ability to help our people in Egoshen. Many in Egoshen over time have accomplished this transformation with the assistance of these guardians and some of the beings from the

Kingdom of Lights. Those having made the transformation have successfully returned to Luminatia. There are still many, many thousands remaining in Egoshen in need of help."

"Winston, please come forward," King Shadel instructed the impending guardian who rose from his chair with his knees feeling a little wobbly, followed by Simon and Yuval. Those seated in the stadium now all held lighted candles. A procession of several hundred green twinkling circled the platform.

"Those are all of our ancestors," Simon whispered into Winston's ear.

As the boy watched the green lights above, one light left the line and approached him. Spinning rapidly before him Myadora emerged from the light. "Hello, Winston," she said softly.

"Myadora!" he exclaimed with delight recognizing her from his Dream of Guardians.

"I'm here to stand with you as you take you oath," she told him as she took his hand in hers.

"Winston," Shadel inquired, "Are you prepared to take the oath and continue your family's legacy."

Glancing in Myadora's eyes and then at Shadel, the young boy asserted, "Yes!" Winston repeated the oath after Shadel, "I, Winston Lane vow to dedicate my life to the service of my King. To use the wisdom and powers that have been bestowed upon me to serve the people who have been taken from Luminatia."

Shadel removed a golden medallion from his pocket and placed it around Winston's neck. "Winston, I entrust you with this medallion and I decree that you are now the newest guardian in the Order of the Light. Welcome Winston," Shadel said as he took the young guardian's hands in his. "As the guardians proceeding you, you will receive instructions from one of the original ten. There is a great deal of training that you must go through before you are able to fulfill your duties."

After the King concluded the induction ceremony, Simon hugged his son as massive explosions of multi colored fireworks lit up the night sky. Winston was astonished by the display. "There are people waiting to meet you," he said as he ushered his son off the platform to a line of guardians clothed in purple and green robes. The first to greet the new guardian was the ten original guardians led by Myadora. Next came the ten who had represented the original during the ceremony.

There she was again, "Pru, it is you. I thought I was seeing things," he exclaimed. "Why are you here?" looking mystified at the sight of his best friend's sister wearing a green robe, "Why are you dressed like that?"

"Cause I'm a guardian," she sighed.

"No, you're just a kid," he blurted out not knowing how to respond.

"Gee thanks," she smiled at his bewilderment, "and what are you, an old man?" she teased.

"Oh yeah, I guess," he said feeling a little stupid at his reaction to Pru as a guardian. "How long have you been a guardian?"

"About eleven months. I'll tell you about it later. See ya," she said as she moved on.

After meeting what seemed like an endless number of guardians and beings from the Kingdom of Lights, Simon brought his son back up to the platform. "Shadel is about to leave, he'd like to say a few words to you."

"You will to do very well as guardian," Shadel declared.

"Thank you, Sir," Winston replied shaking the King's hand still feeling quite overwhelmed by the recent events. "I hope so, but there's so much I don't know."

"That will be taken care of, Myadora will be your teacher and she will teach you whatever you need to know," said Shadel.

"Oh! Staishya won't be my teacher anymore?" he asked feeling the sudden loss of his teacher.

"Staishya will continue as you school teacher. Myadora will teach you the knowledge you will need as a guardian," Shadel replied.

Perplexed at how this would work, "Will Myadora be my teacher after my regular school and how can I explain her to Mother or Willow or my friends?" Winston wanted to know.

"You won't have to explain. Myadora has the power to stop time, which she will do when she comes to teach you." Shadel clarified.

The ministers were at the cottage when Simon and Winston returned at the end of the ceremony. "It's time for you to go back, remember you can't tell anyone about what has happened to you not even your Mother or Willow," his father cautioned him. "I know that will be hard, but it's very important for them not to know."

"What about Pru, she was there?" he questioned.

"Yes, you can discuss this with her, but you need to be watchful that no one is able to hear what you are saying," he advised his son hugging him one last time before they parted.

"I guess, I'm not going to win the scavenger hunt," Winston joked.

"Probably not," his father said with a big grin on his face. "Time will begin again when you return to the outside of the castle. You might feel a little disoriented and find it hard to concentrate for a day or two. You have a lot to absorb. I know you'll do just fine. I love you Winston," he said in parting.

"I love you too Father, when will I see you again," Winston asked feeling a little sad knowing it would be sometime until he actually saw his father again. But now he had a new understanding and compassion for the reasons for their sacrifices.

"In your dreams, my son, I'll see you very soon in your dreams. I'm so proud of you Winston," he said waving as the carriage carrying his son left the cottage to return to the castle.

A great sense of relief came over Winston. He was finally beginning to understand the true nature and importance of his father's secret mission. Helping the people of Egoshen come home. The mystery of the unanswered questions, which troubled him for years, was solved. His father was a guardian and so was he. Winston too, now had a secret he must keep.

CHAPTER TWELVE

One minute he was riding in the carriage and without any warning he was back at the castle sitting on the ground with the man he had just run into. This time he recognized him, "Zachonier, I know you," Winston said standing up and helping Zachonier to his feet. "Were you one of the original ten, you were there?"

"Not quite," he said nodding his head with a twinkle in his eyes, "You'd best get back to your scavenger hunt before you're missed.

"Yes, sir and I'm very sorry for bumping into you," he said as he turned away pulling his next card…find the pond with a rattle and bring a yellow dyniffen petal

The chimes ending the scavenger hunt rang as Winston pulled envelope number '18', he admitted to himself, his father was right, it was really hard to concentrate. He has a secret now, a major one. In the past he had never been able to keep a secret from Willow, but now was about to. He had to. "Am I going to be able to learn everything I need to know to be a good guardian, I'm just twelve?" he wondered tentatively, "What's makes a good guardian?" he did not have a clue. "Maybe Pru would know after all she had been at this for eleven months. Boy, she can keep a secret. What am I worrying about being twelve, she's only eleven. I guess if the King felt I'm ready to be a guardian he must know," he reasoned, muttering to himself.

He met up with Pru after the award ceremony for the scavenger hunt, which neither he nor Pru even came close to winning. Still befuddled by the events of the day, Winston asked Pru "How does it feel to be a guardian?"

"Not really different than before. It's just weird not being able to tell anyone what you are or the things that you've learned. You can only tell your guardian teacher. But now I have you," she said gleefully.

"Can't you talk with your mother or father, you know the one that's a guardian, they're always around," he remarked.

"Well that's the thing, they're actually my adoptive parents. My mother and father went missing when I was a baby and I guess it was before my real mother could become a guardian, so she couldn't be there," Pru sighed sounding a little melancholy. "I do talk to my teacher though. Do you remember when we were on our pirate adventure in the caves the other day?" she asked.

"Yeah!"

"Well my teacher arrived while we were there and she stopped time. It was really, really funny," she laughed.

"What do you mean?" he quizzed.

"Well!" Pru went on, "You had just jumped off this big rock when time stopped, but you hadn't land yet. You just hung in midair. It was very funny. When we finished the class, I had to stand exactly where I was before. You were still hanging and when she left, she put back time and you finished the jump.

"Whoa," Winston said remembering when he saw the flames in the fireplace freeze. "Look, I see Bracer and there's your Chali following right behind him."

"See you in school tomorrow, it's been an interesting day," Pru chuckled as she climbed up atop Chali and headed home.

CHAPTER THIRTEEN

While he waited for Willow to finish getting ready for school, Winston looked over this week's class location schedule. A couple of places really appealed to him, Little Swan Park in particular.

Day 1, literature/creative writing, by the stream leading to the Dapen River
Day 2, mathematics/science at Lever Hall
Day 3, history/geography in meadow near the valley of Prasta
Day 4, meditation/consciousness/art at Varea Falls
Day 5, sport flying/games at Little Swan Park

Their teacher, Staishya always managed to choose great locations for their classes. Since each day was dedicated to a specific subject, she felt it made learning more fun.

"Today's class is literature and creative writing," Winston said, reading off the schedule. "Staishya said we were going to read poetry. Oh! Yuck!" he moaned silently, "that's my very least favorite subject. I think poetry is so boring. It should be just for girls, it's way too sappy for boys." He enjoyed these classes when the material involved stories of a mysterious nature, puzzles or adventures. He was so predictable. Day 5, sport flying. Now that was his favorite class.

It was a short flight from their home on their malgrids to the Dapen River, which ran near the mountains. The twins brought their book reports for their reading assignment "The Wind and the Stone" considered a classic must read for all students.

As the two followed the path next to the river leading to the stream, Winston's focus was on the Ring of Splendor Race semifinals tomorrow. "I wish my father was going be there to see me race," he thought to himself knowing that his father would want that too. "But I understand now why he can't be there and I'm ok with it."

Something had changed in Winston. Ever since becoming a guardian a short time ago, he began to have a deeper perception of his father's mission. Yes, the race was a big deal to Winston, but his new awareness of the importance of the work his father was doing to help the people in Egoshen, to the young guardian, that was foremost. Winston was so proud of his father and his father's dedication to those people.

Yes, he too had taken an oath to dedicate his life to that work. Winston was excited and yet a bit overwhelmed at the prospect of his new future. There was so much he did not know and even more he still needed to learn.

As he continued walking in silence, he reminisced briefly about the time he had just secretly spent with his father and he was grateful for those moments.

Willow finally broke the unusual long silence and said to her brother, "You're usually so talkative. But today, what's up with you? You seem so very far away and really deep in thought. Is everything ok?"

"Nothing much is up, I'm fine, just thinking about tomorrow. It's a big day," Winston replied.

Pru sat alone in the grass near the stream, several yards from the other students and watched as the twins were the last to arrive. Although she was fifteen months younger than Winston, Pru who always seemed wise beyond her years, with strong intuitive abilities could sense when something was bothering him. "What's up, you seem a million miles away?" she asked looking up at him as they waited for their teacher to arrive.

"I've just been thinking about stuff," he said to his young guardian friend as he and Willow sat down next to her. "You know what I mean," he whispered in her ear.

"Yep! Stuff, stuff, I know exactly what you're talking about," she giggled, winking at Winston.

"You're goofy, you know," he said with a smile.

"You bet and proud of it," she laughed.

"She's here," Willow said looking at the large butterfly flying towards them. She admired the beautiful gold and green pattern interwoven in her teacher's white transparent wings. Staishya landed on the grass and began to rapidly spin. Transforming herself into a tall stunning woman in white chiffon dress with the same markings as her butterfly wings. Her golden hair sparkled in the sunlight. "Good morning everyone," she said smiling at her class. "Have you all done your assignment?"

A resounding, "Yes," came from her students.

"Before we begin our class on poetry, let's hear what you've read. Who'd like…"

In mid-sentence everything ceased. There was no movement. Seconds ago, pollen floated freely in the sunlight now it became suspended in midair as the birds hung motionless against the clear blue sky. The river, with its rapid flowing water, came to a halt. Staishya and their classmates froze into statue like beings. All was still. All but Pru and Winston who knew they had entered another dimension where time did not exist. There they were able to remain for what could be perceived, as hours, days or weeks without feeling tired or hungry.

"Myadora," Pru said gleefully as she and Winston watched the tiny globe of light spin until their beautiful ancient teacher appeared.

"Hello, my young guardians, she said greeting her two students as she sat down across from them on a large rock. She wasted no time in beginning their lesson. "Today we'll learn about transformation," she instructed. "But first, let's review. In our past sessions we've looked at how very difficult life is in Egoshen. Winston, can you tell me what is the main cause of the difficulty?"

"Avadon placed veils of illusions in the minds of the people of Egoshen and now the only way they know how to live is in despair filled with negativity," he answered.

"Very good! Pru, what exactly is a veil of illusion?" Myadora asked.

"In Luminatia people know and understand how to live happy, loving and fulfilled lives. It's when their real true memories of how they've lived that kind of positive life are erased from their conscious minds and are replaced with false memories of anger, fear, hatred, misery, pessimism and selfishness. People then believe those false implanted memories are real when in fact they are nothing more than veils of illusions placed in their minds to hide their true memories," Pru answered.

"Excellent, Pru. How are their lives different from Luminatia?" Myadora turned and asked Winston.

Because their minds were filled with dark thoughts it seems the only way they know how to live is in the word you taught us, chaos. In the visions we were shown, people in Egoshen allow their pessimistic emotions and thoughts rule their lives. They're miserable most of the time and filled with anger and jealously. They pretend to be happy. It's like they forgot how to love. Everyone thinks about themselves first, they almost never consider anyone else's feelings." Winston replied

"What were some examples you saw that brought you to this conclusion?" she asked Winston.

He thought for a minute then said, "Well, you showed us a man and woman arguing. The man insisted the woman had to go to his nasty sister's house. She didn't want to go because everyone there was always cruel to her. The man was mean and told her to go. When she kept objecting, he pushed her hard against the wall and she began to cry. Then there was the little boy at the playground being bullied by the three older boys. Nobody came to help him."

"What about you Pru, what did you learn?" she turned to the young girl.

"There's an awful a lot of pretending going on," she said.

"Explain." Myadora asked.

"I remember seeing a man get a promotion at work. Everyone acted like they were happy for him. But when you allowed us to hear what they were really thinking, everyone was jealous and hoped he would mess up and lose his job. They were pretending. Most people on the inside seemed stressed, afraid and depressed. It was as if they felt like victims of life," she said shaking her head. "Those poor people!"

"As guardians, how do you think you can help them?" she quizzed.

"We can go there and teach them how to be happy and tell them there is another way to act and see life. Explain to them they need to begin change their thoughts and actions." Pru answered.

"Pru, if a stranger came to you and said if you stood with you right foot up in the air and smiled, your favorite candy would fall from the sky. Would you believe that person?" Myadora asked.

"No, cause that's silly," she chuckled.

"Why would those people believe you? You're telling them something that in their minds makes no more sense than candy falling from the sky," Myadora explained.

"Well," Pru said "then we'll just have to tell them how Avadon put the veils of illusions in their minds and they forgot how to be happy."

"They've never heard of a veil of illusion nor of Avadon. In Egoshen Avadon has become Manfreed von Neever, their ruler. The people have been brainwashed to believe he can do no wrong and they fear him," she explained.

"Then how do we help them?" Winston asked.

"We'll touch on some methods in today's lesson but we'll go into more details in the future," she explained. "First you must understand when a guardian is sent to Egoshen they must live in the same chaotic environment as the people. In order for a guardian not to succumb to the chaos, we must use our powers of meditation and our medallions for protection."

"What kind of powers do we have," Winston eagerly wanted to know.

"There will be many over time," Myadora answered the eager young boy. "For now, the powers we will touch on are the powers of transformation. Also, some of what is necessary to help Egoshens. In our next sessions we will go in depth, learning more about using those powers of transformations. Also creating illusions, using your intuitive power and telepathic powers. We will touch on blocking your thoughts and the powers of your medallions."

"But we can already communicate with our malgrids telepathically," Pru insisted.

"Yes, but not with other people," Myadora said. "There is much for you to learn and the power of your medallions will help speed up your learning process. There are two types of transformations we'll start to cover today. First is transforming your mind and second is transforming your physical body. This is the beginning of learning the powers you were given as a guardian."

"What do you mean transforming our body? Transforming to what, do you mean like Staishya?" Winston wanted to know.

"To anything you can imagine, not like Staishya. Her species is the Butterflian Shapeshifters and she is only able to transform from a butterfly to a woman and back to a butterfly," his teacher replied. "In Egoshen there will be times when it might be necessary to appear as something other than you. To accomplish the physical transformation, you must first learn to transform your thoughts. Clearing your mind of all negative thoughts such as doubts, fear or anger is vital."

"Doubts about what?" Winston asked.

"Using your powers, for one," Myadora answered.

"I'm a guardian, what difference does it make if I have doubts?" Winston asked.

"For your powers to work, you have to have clarity of mind, great certainty and strong inner energy," replied Myadora.

"How do you clear your mind? My mind always has some kind of thoughts going on. They're not negative just thoughts," asked Pru.

"One way is by meditating on the hieroglyphics in your medallions. It's a very powerful tool for you to use. Only guardians are able to see those hieroglyphics," she explained. "It takes a lot of practice."

"What are the hieroglyphics and why do they work?" asked Winston.

"The hieroglyphics in medallions are a series of secret codes given to each guardian by King Shadel, which allows that guardian to tap into and use some of the King's powers. These powers can only be used for good. When you meditate on the hieroglyphics you ask for the help you need. If your mind is clear, you have certainty and strong inner energy you will get what you need. It might not be what you want, but it will be what you need."

"What do you mean by certainty and strong inner energy?" Winston asked.

"Certainty is the total belief you are able accomplish what is needed, without having any doubts. Strong inner energy is having faith that you possess the ability to tap into some of the King's positive energy force. Without strong inner energy it's hard to have certainty," Myadora told her students. "As I mentioned earlier in Egoshen, guardians must live in the same chaotic environment. The difference is guardians will visibly live a different quality of life without chaos, which will be apparent to those around."

"Guardians begin by treating the people with dignity and kindness. By showing them by example, a different way to live life without judgment and filled only with unconditional love. When they've gained their trust, the guardians can begin to teach the people how to overcome chaos by transforming their negative beliefs. Again, it's a slow process with a lot of resistance from people," Myadora continued.

"As time goes on you will also begin to have the power to see into the future. For now, you are likely to get tiny glimpses. Although you might not quite understand what you're seeing, your visions could seem cloudy and you won't see the complete picture. It's a power that takes many, many years to achieve."

"Until we meet again, I would like you to practice meditating using your medallions. It will also serve to reinforce and speed up your learning process. My dears, I'll see you soon," Myadora said as she stood and spun back into a tiny sphere of light.

As quickly as time appeared to stop, it began. Pru and Winston found themselves back in Staishya class, their teacher in mid-sentence. Willow was raising her hand in response to Staishya's request to report on their homework assignment.

Winston painfully sat through the poetry portion of the class, which felt like an eternity. His thoughts were about the final practice after class for the semi-finals tomorrow. He wondered if Raphaella and Malcolm had practiced enough. In the last two practice sessions they had a difficult time staying in formation. Myan is a natural…she flies as if she was part of her malgrid. Trai was good but Godfrey was the star. Winston knew Godfrey could fly circles around everyone.

"Tomorrow, I believe most of you will find it difficult to concentrate in class, your thoughts will be of the Ring of

Splendor semifinals," Staishya smiled. "This afternoon is your last chance to practice. Have a good practice and enjoy…your malgrids will be here momentarily…until tomorrow then," she said as she transformed back to a butterfly.

CHAPTER FOURTEEN

He never though this day would arrive. Winston paced up and down. "Yep, I'm ready. No, I'm not. Who am I kidding I need more practice," he mumbled to himself. Winston was both nervous and excited. "I'll never get through class today. I think this is gonna be the longest day of my life. Maybe I could stay home and get in some more practice? Right, like mother would allow it and anyhow if I missed class today I wouldn't be allowed to race." It was four o'clock in the morning and he was wide-awake. His alarm would not go off for another three hours. "I wish I could make this day go faster. Hey, I'm a guardian maybe I could use my powers or something. What was I thinking? Right, my powers can't be used to gain something for myself. Get a grip," he told himself anxiously, "you'll be useless if you continue like this." He took his medallion, which hung around his neck and began to meditate. He knew he was allowed to use it for clearing his thoughts and calming down.

Class was finally coming to a close and just as he suspected earlier, the day seemed unending. He listened as Staishya wished them a good game. Watching in the distance as his classmates' malgrids flew towards the clearing near Lever Hall, he did not see Bracer. "Didn't Bracer sense my call?" Winston thought in a panic and then let out a sigh of relief as he saw Bracer flying towards him. He grabbed hold of his bag containing his magenta uniform and ran towards his malgrid wondering if everyone felt as excited as he.

The flight to the stadium near the castle was brief. As he circled the stadium, Winston could see the bleachers on either side of the field beginning to fill. There was a structure at each end of the field. He knew the smaller one housed the equipment used to create the colored firework rings and the thin tower was where the master of the rings would stand. He assumed the larger more ornate structure would be where the King and the various dignitaries would sit. He spotted the six large perches at each end of the field where the malgrids with their riders would wait for their turn in the race. As he got closer, he noticed the two banners. One over each set of bleachers. To the right was the orange and yellow banner for the opponent's team, the Raysmins and to the left was the magenta and green banner for his team, the Squines.

Winston circled the field one more time before Bracer landed in the Squines holding area. Then he headed to the locker room to change.

"Raysmins warm up time is now over. Ten minutes until the Squines warm up time," a voice announced over the loud speaker.

Godfrey, captain of the Squines signaled for his teammates to mount their malgrids. "Myan, Trai, Winston, Raphaella, Malcolm are we all ready to show these Raysmins how to maneuver, fly right, tight and win? Are we going to the finals?" Godfrey shouted with a great burst of enthusiasm.

"Yes!" they screamed back as one by one they took off for a last practice flight before the race. An air of excitement and confidence permeated the team. Earlier a unanimous decision was made by the Squines not to watch the Raysmins warm up since the Raysmins were favored to win they did not want to lose their confidence.

Thirty minutes later a voice over the loud speaker proclaimed, "Raysmins, Squines, The Ancient One, King Shadel has arrived. The Ring of Splendor Race is about to begin. Racers please take your place on your designated perches." The spectators in the bleachers began clapped and whistled while the racers waved to the King as they flew to their perches. Once on their appropriate perches, the voice announced "Racers, the screens will now rise in front of you with your individual sequence and sizes of twenty-four colored rings which you will be required to fly through, you have exactly five minutes to commit this information to memory. When the gong sounds team captains, Godfrey and Aina, will fly to the master of the rings. There they must retrieve their gold ring. This will be held in the master's out stretched arms. Once a captain has their ring, they will begin the race.

Winston sat on Bracer and watched as his best friend flew with great precision towards the tower. First flying straight, then a sharp turn to the side enabling him to fly close enough to the master of the rings with one arm stretched up above his head to grab his ring as he held on tight to his malgrid with his other arm. Winston knew it was a difficult and dangerous maneuver. Too close or the wrong angle would result in the master being knocked off the tower. Not close enough would require another pass and a loss of precious time. But Godfrey was good and had practice long hours. He got the ring on the first pass, seconds before the favorite Aina.

"Wow" he said aloud, as the stunning explosions became visible in the sky. It was like witnessing a fireworks display. Only the fireworks were shaped into perfect rings, which each skillful racer attempted to fly through. The sky was filled with hundreds of bursting rings in various sizes and brilliant colors all appearing in different directions. He stared straight at Godfrey and was fascinated by his friend's remarkable ability to maneuver through his sequence of rings with seeming ease. The earlier rings began to fade while others continued to explode in the sky. His heart pounded in his chest as he tried to calm himself down. He needs to be calm and focused he was the sixth and last racer on his team. It would be a while before his turn came.

Willow screamed from the bleachers, "Go Malcolm!" As he and his malgrid left the perch, heading straight up to his first ring. She had a secret crush on him and blushed a bit at her unanticipated enthusiastic outburst. To her delight he passed through with ease. She looked up as he made a severe left turn heading towards his next ring when Lanc, a racer from the Raysmins made a sharp right turn and nearly collided with him. This forced Malcolm into an unexpected upside-down maneuver causing him to lose his seating and began to slip off Langi. Panicked she put her hands over her eyes afraid of what she was about to see.

"It's ok," Pru whispered in her ear as she gently pulled Willow's hand from her eyes. "Malcolm's fine, Langi did a fast rollover and got Malcolm seated."

Anessa, who sat in the bleachers next to Willow's other side, put her arm around her visibly shaken daughter, "Honey, he really is ok, he recovered beautifully." Trying to distract her daughter from the near disaster involving the boy she sensed Willow liked, Anessa remarked, "I can visualize a myriad of riders on their malgrids of flying through those exquisite rings in my next painting. What do you think?"

Feeling a little calmer, she answered, "Mother, I think that would be wonderful." The remainder of Malcolm's performance was adequate and uneventful to Willow's satisfaction.

Winston was up the Squines were behind. He felt apprehensive, his palms were clammy and his hands began to shake. "If I don't do better than my best, we've lost. Oh! I don't want this responsibility. I'm not a good enough racer," he thought. Myan was finishing her portion of the race and would shortly swoop down to pass him the gold ring. As he did before every race or game he participated in, he scanned the bleachers once again wishing and hoping that his father would be there to see him race. He saw his mother and sister. Pru sat with her family next to Willow, but his father was not there.

Winston glanced over to where King Shadel was sitting. It was a thrill to have him there. But in that instant his heart seemed to stop. His lungs could not get air. He closed his eyes, what was he seeing? Two holograms were seated to the left and right of the King. He rubbed his eyes; he could not hold back the tears. It was his father and Myadora. His father had come. It did not matter to him that his father appeared in the form of a hologram that no one else could see. He was there and he was going to see Winston race.

In his peripheral vision he caught a glimmer of something flying towards him. For a brief moment he blocked out everything. He just stared filled with elation at the sight of his father.

"The ring!" his brain began to function again. It took but a second for everything to come back into focus. Myan was flying towards him in an upside-down maneuver. Her arm extended over her head. In her hand was the gold ring, which he needed to grab in order to begin his leg of the race. A tinge of panic set in. She's so close, is it too late. Did I lose focus for too long?" he did not dare to breath, his arm just shot up above his head and grabbed the ring.

Winston heard the crowd cheer as he and Bracer took off and shot straight up towards the sky. Six rings exploded above in different directions; blue, plum, pink, lavender, violet, green. He thought fast. Blue and lavender were the first two in the sequences. He guided Bracer through the large sparkling blue ring then heading downward and making a sharp right turn eased through the lavender. A slight distance away another series of six rings appeared yellow, green, blue, fuchsia, turquoise and orange. "Come on boy," he said to Bracer, "its turquoise, blue then fuchsia" as they flew through the turquoise, made a sharp upside-down loop through the blue and a quick sideward turn left into the fuchsia. Winston imbued with an intense feeling of confidence as he caught a glimpse of Jax, his opponent who seemed to hesitate as she approached a ring. But there was no time to think or watch another racer, only to focus on his rings and sequences. He knew with each series of rings the degree of difficulty would increase. Colors would be similar; sizes would vary and angle to maneuver would require more intense concentration and skill. In the next two sets he only missed one ring. He was doing well.

The next series exploded. There were ten rings. They seemed to be all over the sky. "Oh!" he said out loud as a sudden feeling of trepidation hit the pit of his stomach. "Some of these colors are almost the same and the angle of the rings, whoa." He took a deep breath, "I can do it, I can do it," he repeated to himself as his confidence returned. "Come on Bracer, old boy, we just need to get through five," he shouted as his heart raced in his chest. The first two seemed simple as they headed towards the silver rings. There were two sizes and were far apart. It was hard to judge. "The furthest one, that's the right one," he determined and raced towards it. As soon as he flew into the ring, he knew it was not the right one. "No time to guess," he told himself as he guided Bracer into an upside-down maneuver and into a sharp turn to the left towards the red ring. "Made it! One more, Bracer, we need this one," he said as he lowered his body close to his malgrid to pick up speed. Time was running out, some of the rings were fading. There it was, down below and to the right, the aquamarine ring, he could see it. It was beginning to fade; he was not going to make it and it was gone. Disappointment flooded through him, his team was behind and he had not helped.

Winston could feel the adrenaline pulsating through his body. There was one more set and this was the most difficult, both racers rings would be intermingled.

Twenty brilliant colored sparking rings shot up into the sky. Each racer needed to pass through five rings in the sequence.

Pru watched as Winston maneuvered past Jax and into his first ring. Jax rolled over to make her first ring. Her malgrid's wing hit the edge, no point. Pru cheered, the Squines were behind by four points and that error helped them. Her eyes were fixed on her friend who nearly collided with Jax as he made a wide loop heading to his second ring. He missed it and Pru groaned. She held her breath as both racers conquered their next rings. Jax's next ring faded before she could reach it. With two rings to go for each racer, Pru screamed, "Come on Winston you've got it in you, you can do it." Both racers failed to make the next ring. They were still one point behind as Pru grabbed Willow's hand and nervously held on tight knowing that the last ring was worth three points.

Winston felt light headed, his heart pounded, as perspiration seemed to drip from his entire body. He did not think; he just reacted as he began the most difficult maneuver of the race towards the radiant gold ring. A large loop to the left, straight down past the cluster of crimson and blue rings, another loop around the green and fuchsia rings, there it was his last ring, and there was Jax flying right next to him towards her ring. They approached their ring on target with great speed. Closing his eyes, he gave Bracer the signal to go for it. He heard screams from below. "Was it for his team or for the Raysmins? Did they both make? He didn't know."

Pru and Willow squealed at the sight of Winston's triumphant score, Jax once again nicked the ring with her malgrid's wing and the Squines won.

Winston looked down and witnessed the elation of his teammates and knew. He looked towards the King and saw his father cheering. His heart was full as tears flowed down his cheeks. His father was there.

CHAPTER FIFTEEN

It was two o'clock in the morning when Godfrey looked at the clock again. "I'm still not sleeping," he said aloud as adrenalin surged through his body. He had tossed and turned since he went to bed at eleven p.m. Normally, he would fall asleep as soon as his head hit the pillow. Not tonight. The only thing his mind was able to focus on over and over was they made it to the finals; he kept revisiting the highlights of the race. "Winston really came through for the team. I didn't think he had it in him. Wow, he was great," he could see his best friend in his mind's eye as he went through the last gold ring. He had never seen Winston in such good form. "That's it! I can't lie in bed any longer," he said jumping up and putting on his clothes.

Godfrey knew he was not supposed to go into the tunnels at night, but tonight was different. He was so excited he was unable sleep. There was all this excess energy flowing through him and he needed to do something to wear it off and help calm him down. Carefully he made his way down the back staircase leading to a passage into the tunnels beneath his house. "I'm gonna be thirteen in four months. I'm not a kid anymore," he rationalized. "My parents will understand they'll be ok with this. Besides I'm only go into the tunnels with the painted yellow fluorescent line along the walls," he thought, knowing his father had painted it so the children would know where they were permitted to go and it enabled them to keep from getting lost. As long as they followed the line it would lead them to a safe exit.

He lit the lantern at the entrance of the tunnel. The idea was exhilarating. He had never been in the tunnels alone at night. "Oh wow! This can be great," Godfrey said as he looked around at the empty tunnel with all of its imaginary possibilities. "I can do a pirate adventure by myself. I'll be a pirate that escapes from my favorite nemeses, the hideous Captain Higola, who stole and hid the magical sword of the Myta. I'm going on a quest to find it," he said in an exaggerated voice.

He wandered around the tunnels climbing up onto ledges and poking behind boulders while pretending to look for the magical sword. Godfrey was aware of the dangerous tunnels they were marked by signs: DANGER, DO NOT ENTER.

"Hmm! What's that?" he whispered as the light from his lantern reflected off an object wedged in a large pile of rocks. "Oooo! That looks interesting," he said as went to investigate. "Whatever it is, it's very sparkly." Fascinated, he climbed to the top of the pile and started removing rocks to reach the object. The heavier rocks he let roll down the pile. The ones he could manage to lift, he tossed. It was hard work and there seemed to be more rocks covering the object, but he was determined.

It was then he heard a loud rumbling sound. "Oh, crumb buckets…this is not a good thing," he shouted as he jumped off the pile of rocks. Godfrey's instincts told him what was happening. Part of the tunnel was caving in and he needed to run to safety. He darted around a corner into another tunnel. Tripping over a rock, his lantern flew out of his hand and the oil, which fueled it spilled over the ground. He stood there in the dark, a victim of the rockslide. As he hugged the wall of a new tunnel all he could see was black. His heart pounded and his knees felt as if they had turned to rubber. The rumbling had stopped. He slumped to the ground remembering the candle and matches in his pocket his father always insisted they take with them as a safety precaution whenever they went into the tunnels. He never imagined he would ever need to use them. Lighting it, he could see the dust in the air as he peered around. "Why did I come down here?" he blurted out with regret. "When

I get out of here, I know I'm going to get a major lecture from my father insisting I should have known better," he predicted as the feeling of fear crept through his body. Shaking he realized he was in an unmarked tunnel. How was he going to get out he queried nervously, knowing that these tunnels went on for miles? Stories were told of people getting lost and never finding their way out. "Could they be true? I'm never going to get out? I'm being ridiculous," he told himself.

After walking about a mile, he began to smell fresh air and headed in that direction. "Halleluiah, I finally made it, I'm out. Whoa!" he said with a sigh of relief as he walked towards the opening.

What the h…! Oh, father it's you, for a minute I thought I was seeing something very weird. I thought you were some sort of hideous monster. Wow, I guess my eyes were playing tricks on me," he declared with a sigh of relief as he ran to hug his father. "I'm so sorry, I know I shouldn't have gone down into the tunnels. It was scary. I promise I've learned my lessons the hard way."

CHAPTER SIXTEEN

It was a combination of hearing the sound of pebbles hitting his window and what seemed like Pru's voice in his head frantically calling his name that woke Winston with a jolt. "What the…" he said disoriented as he sat up in bed rubbing his ears not sure if what he was hearing had come from a dream. There was that sound again, it was pebbles hitting the glass. He ran to the window and saw Pru down below.

She put her finger to her mouth motioning for him to be quiet while waving for him to come down.

He threw on his clothes and rushed down to meet her. "What's the matter?" he asked with concern as he stared at the tears running down her cheeks.

"It's Godfrey, they've got him," she sobbed.

"Who's got him?"

"Avadon's monsters," she blurted.

"What? When?" shocked by what he was hearing.

"We can't talk here," she said

"Ok," he thought for a minute then summoned Bracer with his mind. "Let's go to the cave near Mount Rimpar. I just need to leave a note, I'll be a second," he said running back into the house. He glanced at the clock in the kitchen, six am. His mother and Willow wouldn't be up for another hour and a half.

"Mother,
Woke up early and felt like going flying with Bracer, see you later…
W"

"Are you sure?" Winston asked as he sat on the ground next to Pru outside of the cave.

"Yes, I must have woken up a little while after they took him because I could sense something was wrong. I went to his room and he wasn't there. So, I went to look for him. I checked all through the house and saw the door leading to the tunnels was left open. He always leaves it open if he goes down there through the house. Winston I could feel he's not here," she explained.

Winston understood what she was saying. Ever since becoming a guardian he was beginning to have a strong intuitive sense and knew she was right. Avadon's creatures had taken Godfrey. "Do your parents know?"

"No, I didn't have the heart to wake them up and tell them. And if I did, they'd want to know how I knew. You know I couldn't tell them it's because I'm a guardian. The King's minister will be coming in a few hours to break the news to them. Winston what are we going to do, they've got Godfrey?" she sobbed.

"Oh Pru, I don't know what we can do," he said as tears rolled down his face. He put his arm around his sobbing friend.

CHAPTER SEVENTEEN

It had been three weeks since Godfrey was taken. Pru's heart was heavy as she grieved for her brother. There was emptiness inside of her. It felt as though a piece of her was missing. Her parents now seemed to exist in a robotic state and she could feel their great pain. The King's minister came to the house each evening in an attempt to counsel the family. He tried to assure them their pain would lessen in time. But Pru was not buying that. She kept thinking there had to be something she could do to bring Godfrey back. Her pain lessening in time was not acceptable.

Pru took solace in the reality that she and Winston grew closer. He missed Godfrey almost as much as she did. Although their learning curve with Myadora had accelerated during the past weeks it was not enough to keep their young minds off Godfrey.

"I know this a very difficult time for both of you, it's so unusual for a youngster to be taken," affirmed Myadora with the deepest of sympathy. "But your focus must be on the teachings for now, so when you're older and have learned all that's necessary, you will be able to go to Egoshen to help rescue those like Godfrey or perhaps even Godfrey.

"Why can't we go now?" Pru insisted, as Winston looked stunned at her ridiculous comment.

"First, because it is very dangerous even when a guardian completes their studies, which you have not. You're much too young to shoulder that kind of responsibility. One has to be at least twenty-one years old before they are even considered for service in Egoshen. An experienced guardian from the Kingdom of Lights is then assigned to them for a training period. For the next several years they accompany that guardian to Egoshen for a series of short visits," Myadora explained.

"Oh!" Pru said disappointed at what she had just heard.

Willow understood Pru's need to spend more alone time with Winston, as she watched the pair wander off together after class. She did not even want to imagine what life would be like without her twin and was happy knowing her brother was there for Pru.

"I think we should go to Egoshen," Pru announced to Winston as they walked along the path towards the clearing.

He was astounded at what he was hearing, "Are you nuts? Didn't you hear what Myadora told us earlier?"

"Yeah!" she hesitated. "But you don't see the pain my parents are in every day and it's not getting easier. And I don't want to wait years until I can see my brother, I want him here now. Don't you Winston?"

"Of course, I want him back, Pru you're eleven and I'm twelve," he said wanting things to be different. "I wish we could do something, but we can't."

"Yes, we can, I know we can," she emphatically insisted. "Besides you love adventures and this could be the adventure of a lifetime. I know if it was you or me in Egoshen, Godfrey do everything to help us."

It scared him. She was beginning to make sense. He knew his friend would try to move mountains to help him. "First of all, we don't know where to find the secret window that leads to Egoshen."

"Yes, we kinda do if you think about it. We've got a lot of clues. Remember when Myadora showed the visions of Avadon taking the people through the secret window. We know what it looks like. We can find it I know we can. I'm sure it's somewhere near the Queen Suri's cottage in the forest," Pru reminded him.

"Well the next problem is we can only go through the window two hours before daybreak of the new moon. If we're outside in the streets then Avadon's creepy things will get us," he told her thinking this is never going to work.

"Well, we won't be in the streets," she answered with a smile on her face.

It was the first time he had seen her smile in three weeks, "What are you talking about? How can we get to the secret window without being outside on the ground at that time?" he asked, puzzled by her statement.

"We start flying on our malgrids before the two hours and watch from above for those creepy things to come through the window. Once they're out of sight we can fly over the window. Then climb down on a rope from our malgrids. That way we just never touch the ground. It can work, I know it can," Pru said confidently.

"She really can't believe we can do this. But she's definitely got what seems be the right answers," he thought. He knew if it had been Willow who was taken, he would do everything he could think of to get her back.

"We've got a little under a week to get ready and a lot to do. We just have to keep flying over the area until we see it, we know what we're looking for," she said feeling relief she was going to be able to do something to bring her brother home. She was certain they would find the secret window. She could close her eyes and see it in Myadora's vision.

"Maybe this isn't so crazy," he thought. "Well actually, yes, it is," but he knew he needed to do this. Godfrey was his best friend.

CHAPTER EIGHTEEN

Other than the fact they kept the secret they were guardians, neither Winston nor Pru had ever-outright lied to their parents. They each said they were spending a few nights at a friend's home for some special event. Their trusting parents had no reason to doubt them. Lying was an extremely uncomfortable feeling for both of them, but they agreed the reason for the deception was justified. After all they were going to save Godfrey.

Winston and Pru waited anxiously in the still night air with their malgrids perched at the top of one of the highest trees in the forest. They had been there since two thirty a.m. The only sound was an old hoot owl that seemed to be watching them from the adjacent tree. Each felt as though swarms of butterflies fluttered in the pit of their stomachs. Through Myadora's visions they learned Avadon's creatures always came through the secret window at three thirty a.m. To be safe the two decided to remain in the tree until three fifteen a.m. at which time they would quietly fly over the secret window.

"It's time," Winston announced.

"Let's go," she responded in a quivering voice as they each signaled their malgrids to take off.

It took them a few minutes to reach their destination, which Winston had finally located two days earlier.

Winston had been determined to find its location. From the visions shown him by Myadora, closing his eyes he could picture the surrounding area of the location of the secret window. He flew over the forest every day for almost a week until he recognized what he thought was the configuration of trees, which hid the window. Jubilant at the possibility of his finding and careful to notice that no one was about, he and Bracer landed to survey the site. Hidden behind a familiar but almost impenetrable cluster of bushes and covered with dense hanging ivy, Winston saw it. Placed two feet off the ground was a simple multi-paned wooden framed window with a tarnished brass latch in the center when unlatched allowed the window to open into Luminatia. It seemed to be only large enough to permit one man to go through at a time and he wonder how long must it have taken for all those people Avadon took with him to pass through.

They flew over the site in silence anticipating the arrival of Avadon's creatures but nothing could have prepared them for what they were about to experience.

At precisely three thirty a.m. an eerie brownish green light began to emanate though the bushes below as the bushes seemed to disappear into the ground. The secret window's width quadrupled in size and the height grew to about twenty feet, as it swung open. A chill ran up Winston spine, his eyes opened so wide at the sight before him he thought they would pop out of their sockets. Pru cringed and put her hand over her mouth in an attempt to muffle any shriek she might make. There they were, three harufanks more terrifying and hideous than anything they had seen in the vision. These were real.

Their long thick cylindrical bodies slithered out from the window and onto the ground. Pus like ooze ran from their rough scaled skin covering their huge snake like bodies. Pru gasped at the sight of the four layers of large razor-sharp fangs extending from the jaws of their ghastly repulsive dragon face. A coiled horn protruded from the center of their forehead, the pincer at the end of the tails seemed to grab at the air as they moved. The beasts' lime green bodies glisten in the darkness as if they were filled with electricity.

The brazen harufanks let out a horrific ear-piercing sound announcing their arrival in Luminatia. Raising the top two thirds of their eighteen-foot bodies off the ground, Pru winced as they each revealed two arm-like extremities with pincers instead hands. Their bodies now vertical, continued to slither away from the window on their tails.

Winston gagged as the fetid stench of these three monsters reached his nostrils.

Bracer and Chali raced upward in an attempt take their riders away from that disgusting odor, but it followed them. Winston and Pru watched with revulsion as the harufanks disappeared from sight.

After waiting a few extra minutes to make sure they were safe. The young guardians instructed their aeropaths to hover over the window as they lowered the knotted ropes anchored around their malgrids' neck, knowing the only way they could be detected by these evil creatures was if any part of their body touched the ground. Careful to keep the ropes off the ground the two slid off their malgrids and began to climb down towards the entrance to the window when they noticed it was beginning to close.

With their hearts beating so rapidly they could barely breath, Winston and Pru descended the ropes at lightning speed. They had been under the belief that the window stayed open until the hurafunks returned and did not count on it closing. What would they do if it closed? There was no time for thinking just reacting.

"Hurry, swing the rope towards the window and jump, now," Winston instructed in a loud fervent whispered voice as they were now level with the entrance where the window opening was only two feet wide.

In the past Pru had mastered pumping and jumping off a swing, but never aiming her landing in a particular place, "No time for doubt," she whispered to herself aloud. "Ready, aim, fire," she said hurling herself through the opening followed by Winston who nearly landed on top of her.

CHAPTER NINETEEN

"Wow! We made it, we're in," Winston said with a sigh of relief. "Pru are you ok?" he asked as they sat in pitch darkness.

"I'm ok, I think," she said reaching into her backpack for her torchlight. "Boy it stinks in here it smells like awful mold."

"Yeah, but not as smelly as those disgusting harufanks," Winston said shinning his torchlight, he had just flicked on, about the walls and ceiling of the damp cave which seemed to be covered in some sort of black glistening vines.

"This place doesn't only stink but it's really creepy," Pru said looking down at the caves floor. Yuck! The floor is covered in muddy slims, oooh disgusting," she moaned pulling her foot out of the muck she had just stepped into.

"Is that all you can do," he said with a wry smile on his face, "is complain?" as they started to explore the cave. "Are you going girly on me? You used to be such a rough and tumbler."

"No, I'm not going girly," she muttered. "Oh, like you like this place," she snipped jokingly. The sound of a crackling noise similar to the snapping of twigs interrupted the banter. "What's that?" Pru said startled at the odd sound that broke the silence of the cave.

"I don't know," Winston replied feeling unnerved as the cave began to come alive with more eerie sounds, whooshing; shrieking; scratching; cackling.

"Don't like this," Pru said grabbing hold of Winston's arm not knowing what or who was making those noises.

"Look" he said pointing his torchlight at the entrance of what appeared to be a tunnel. "It's probably just echoes coming from there," he replied as he tried to reassure Pru, although he felt as if he wanted turn and run but there was not where to run. "Ok it's time to suck it up. We've gotta get a grip. It looks like we're gonna have to go through the tunnel. There doesn't seem to be any other way to go," Winston insisted. "Not everything goes bump in the night."

"There's always home," she sighed. "And how do you know something isn't going to go bump?"

"Do you want to go home?" he asked.

"No," Pru said in a whispered voice. "We've gotta find Godfrey, I'm ok, really. Let's go," she said regaining some semblance of composure.

"Are you sure?" he asked.

"Yeah," she said taking a deep breath, "let's hit the tunnel."

Winston took her hand in his and gave it a hard, reassuring squeeze. "We're gonna be just fine," he said leading her into the tunnel, trying to convince himself as well as her.

Once inside the tunnel it became very warm. The air was heavy and still reeked from the stench of mold making breathing uncomfortable. Pru felt as though her lungs were made of clay and breathing became a chore instead of something she took for granted. She looked at Winston, he was panting. Perspiration ran down the side of his face and she knew he was probably having as much difficulty breathing as she.

The mud covering the slimy tunnel floor was slippery and thick. Pru let out a squeal as she lost her balance and started to slip and fall into the muck. Reacting quickly, Winston grabbed her arm and broke her fall. "Oh wow, thanks," she whimpered, "the idea of falling into this warm sickening goop makes my skin crawl. It's bad enough having to step in it."

"Yeah! It makes my skin crawl too." He had known her and seen her almost every day since she was only a couple of months old but he had never really looked at her before. She was a wisp of a girl, thin and petite unlike himself who he considered to be solid. He did not think of himself as fat because he was not, but neither was he thin, he thought of himself as something in between. He was happy with being solid. And he felt being solid would help him somehow keep Pru safe in this miserable tunnel. The atmosphere in this tunnel made him feel like he needed to retch and he thought if he felt that way, he could not even begin to imagine what Pru was going through. All he knew is he wanted to and had to protect her. She seemed so vulnerable. "Let's stay close to the wall. I'm not going to let you fall again," he said as his legs seemed to slip out from under him and he fell backwards into the slimy muck.

Pru gasped. "Oh! Are you ok?" aiming her torchlight at Winston who was now covered in slimy mud.

"Yeah, I'm just great," he said with a slight tone of sarcasm in his voice.

"Look at you. You're a mess, I can't take you anywhere," she laughed in an attempt to break the tension.

"Oh yeah," he said pulling himself up. "Well take a look at you," he smiled wiping a little muck on the tip of her nose with his finger.

"I've got a couple of pairs of gardener's gloves in my sack. I think if we put them on, we'll be able to grab the vines on the wall and keep our butts out of the muck," Pru said wiping the mud from her nose.

"Aren't you the one prepared for a rainy day," he teased putting on the gloves and thinking, "so much for being her protector."

The slimy black vines seemed to have multiplied as the pair continued through the tunnel. The vines crept up the up the walls to the ceiling and then hung down like huge clusters of elongated worms brushing against Pru and Winston's faces. "Can it get any more disgusting?" Pru groaned pushing them out of the way.

"I hope not," Winston grunted.

"I just want to get out of here already and get to the other side. The further we go into this tunnel, it seems the worse it gets," Pru said losing patience with her surroundings when a three inch spider like Cyclops with a slimy substance oozing from its only eye and it's jagged razor sharp tongue whipping in and out of its mouth crawled onto her arm omitting its own vile pungent odor. Her eyes widened in horror as the creature stared and hissed at her. Holding back a scream, she stood frozen to the spot.

Instinctively Winston reacted. Clenching his fist, he punched the spider with such force that it went flying across to the other side of the tunnel. His hand was dripping with the ooze from the spider. It was so repulsed he began to shake.

Pru stood next to him, the color drained from her face. She remained motionless, unable to move. Her glazed eyes stared into space. Fear rose from the pit of his stomach as he thought, "Did the spider bite her? Is she paralyzed? Why isn't she moving?" Desperately he tried to compose himself. "Pru, Pru," he shouted in a whispered voice afraid that some other creature would hear him. His heart pounded in his chest, "Pru answer me. Are you ok?"

Breath and movement returned to her body. "No, I'm not! I want to get out of here now," she emphatically insisted, her body trembling as she wiped away the tears running down her cheeks.

"Did that thing bite you?" he nervously asked.

"No, I just want to get out of here," she repeated. "It seems like everything here stinks and oozes. It's disgusting."

"Yeah, you're right, it's disgusting. I think we're almost there," he said encouragingly trying to keep her spirits up, but not really knowing when or if the tunnel would end. "Come on, we've gotta keep going." He took her hand as they continued to make their way through the tunnel.

"Three tunnels!" exclaimed Pru as they stood before a fork leading in three directions.

"Oh great! Now what do we do?" Winston said shaking his head in frustration at the latest obstacle confronting them. "Ok Pru, what do you think, which one?"

"Don't know. Let's go with the driest one and hopefully one that doesn't stink," she said trying to interject some humor to break the mounting tension they both felt.

"Terrific and which one would that be?" he said with a slight sound of sarcasm in his voice.

"Don't know," she said exasperated, "let's go for the middle one."

"I guess that's as good a choice as any," he sighed looking at the three similar tunnels.

"Ok here goes," Pru said taking the lead determined to get out of their present surroundings. After a while of trudging through that tunnel, Pru said in an excited whisper, "I think I see a light up ahead? You see it?" she gasped. "You think that's it, the end of the tunnel?"

"I don't know, it could be," he said straining his eyes at the dot of light ahead. "Yeah! Let's go for it," he said as he headed towards the light. The tunnel floor was dry and the vines became less dense which made walking easier.

The dot of light grew, as they got closer, "Winston," she sighed impatiently, "I think we're finally getting out of this revolting place."

Pru was about two yards ahead of him. He let her lead the way so that he could keep her in his line of sight. Suddenly, she came to an abrupt stop. "What's the matter now?" Winston asked.

"Look!" she said pointing her torchlight at what looked like an oily pool of water covering the ground ahead. "It doesn't look like we can go around it. What if it's deep? How are we going to get through it?"

"Maybe it's not deep, come on don't be negative, let's check it out," he said walking to the edge of the water. He looked around for some sort of stick that he could measure the depth, there was none. He knelt down, rolled up his sleeve and was about to put his arm into the water to determine its depth.

"What are you doing?" Pru asked with fervor when she realized what Winston was about to do. "Are you crazy, you don't know what's in there?"

"Do you have a better idea?" he said extending his arm into the water. "Yikes!" he shouted a moment later and quickly pulled his arm out of the water. It was covered with three, four-inch, thick-bodied black leach like creatures. "Pru, they won't come off," he shrieked shaking his arm and violently rubbing it against the wall. "They feel like they're eating into my arm."

Pru began to hit them with her torchlight, but nothing happened. "Winston, hold on I've got an idea," she said pulling a candle and some matches from her sack. Lighting the candle, she touched the flame to the flesh eaters and one by one they fell off. "Are you ok?"

"Just when you think you can't get grossed out any more…" his voice trailed off.

"Yeah! I don't even want to consider that thought," she shrugged. "But how are we going to get across?"

He surveyed the dilemma in front of them for a few minutes and then taking a deep breath and letting it go, "The water seems to go down the tunnel for about fifteen feet or so, the only way across is to climb up on the walls. We can hold onto the vines for support and work our way along the wall until we get past the water or whatever this stuff is."

"What are we, monkeys? And if we slip, then what?" she wanted to know.

"We're not gonna slip, we're gonna do it, Pru we have to have certainty. It's the only way across," he contended.

"Oh boy certainty in this mess, you're kidding. No, you're not," she sighed. Ok! Right, certainty it is," she snapped. Closing her eyes, she attempted to physic herself up for the task ahead. She stood there for a few minutes contemplating what they had been through and what they needed to do. "You know Winston, when we get out of here, I'm gonna need to take a very, very long hot bubble bath to wash this disgusting tunnel off me," she quipped as she reached for a vine on the wall and began the crossing.

"I think you're getting girly on me again? Only you could think of a bath at a time like this," Winston sighed, feeling a bit of the enormous tension had been broken. Following Pru, he grabbed a vine and said watching her, "You're doing real good Pru, keep going, we're almost there."

She could see it, another two feet and ahead was solid ground. Careful and moving slowly, she made it. The pool of slime with those grossly disgusting creatures was behind her as she climbed down the wall. Her feet were on solid ground. Pru looked back and saw Winston following a short distance behind her. "Hallelujah, we're out of this miserable repulsive tunnel," she said looking at Winston who was completely covered in dirt and grime. "You're a mess," she laughed.

"Well, I wouldn't look in a mirror just yet if I were you," he teased, his eyes inspecting their surroundings. He looked up at the gray sky and around at a forest of seemingly endless dead trees. Many of the trees had broken trunks and branches. Lifeless brown vines covered some of the trees. An eerie silence permeated the air. There were no sounds of birds or animals or any other signs of life.

"Winston, what do we do now?" Pru whispered hesitantly looking about.

"I'm not sure," he answered. "Let's just get away from the cave, but since it all looks alike now, we better leave some sort of markings so we can find our way back."

"Yeah! But what can we use that no one would notice?" she asked.

He thought for a minute, "those funny knots Staishya showed us. Do you remember?"

"Yeah, she called it the bunger knot," she reminded him.

"The vines," he pointed. "We can tie a bunch of the vines into those knots. They're so funny looking, if someone sees them, they're gonna think the vines just grew that way."

"You're a genius," she said with a smile.

"Yes, I am," he joking proclaimed as he walked over to a tree and began knotting the vines.

CHAPTER TWENTY

They came to a clearing when they neared the end of the dead and decaying forest. It offered no cover for them, just a few rocks and boulders up ahead. Seeing no one, they decide to venture cautiously into the clearing. Ear piercing screeching and howling erupted in the distance. Shaken, they looked around and saw nothing.

"Run, get back to the forest quick. We need to get up into a tree," Winston shouted as he spotted a pack of hideous looking creatures running towards them.

They scrambled up a tree with not a second to spare. Winston and Pru straddled a branch about twelve feet off the ground. These ferocious creatures were now at the base of the tree taunting the young guardians. They were peculiar huge animals that seemed to be part scraggly dog with their heads resembling a deformed gorilla. Their teeth were pointy and looked razor sharp.

"What are we going to do?" Pru asked terrified at what she was seeing.

"I don't know, I don't know," he repeated in anguish. "I think we're safe up here for now, but we can't climb any higher."

Then startled, as seemingly out of nowhere, emerged a very odd, disfigured, little man who jumped out from behind a cluster of dead bushes. Following him were two fierce horrid looking creatures. He had a tight grip on their leashes. These were the same species of creatures that were trying to attack them. There was a whip with six lashes attached to the handle hanging on a hook at the man's waist. He took the whip into his hand and began to strike the ground while yelling at these creatures. They immediately ran off into the forest.

"Ya can come down now, ya be safe," the little man advised them. He saw the shocked look on the faces of the two guardians as they gawked at these creatures and said "Them be Keworgles, ya never seen one before, they'rrre real mean." Under the impression Winston and Pru were from Egoshen he said, "I doon't know whoo ya are, but ya comin wit me. Yooou twoo are gonnabe worken foor meeee, and if ya gimme any trouble, I'm letten my two friends here have at ya." he said in a slow, eerie, whining, nasal voice.

As they carefully climbed down the tree, they found this man frightening. Strong feelings of utter fear and despair welled up inside of Winston and Pru. They had never experienced such intense negativity before. A voice within each guardian instructed them "Don't give in to these feelings. You're under the influences of Egoshen. It's part of the illusion."

"What's your name?" Pru asks the ugly stranger while trying to appear calm.

"I'm called Wank," he whined. The odd little man asked them, "And what doooo they call yooou?"

Not wanting to give their real names Winston replied, "I'm Will and this is my sister Willameena."

"Yooou come with meee," Wank snorted. "I've goot a looot of woork foor yooou tooo doo. I loost my Brinta, she ran away. If you try the Keworgles will get ya."

They walked for about a mile through a muddy, murky swamp until they came to a filthy, old, dilapidated shack.

"I want yooou tooo make this place clean, nice," Wank ordered them as he snickered maliciously.

As he tied his Keworgles to a post he gave them an order, "Make sure they doon't run away like the others, or I will make soooup out of yoooou, very delicious Keworgle soooup."

Winston and Pru were being held prisoners by Wank, scrubbing and cleaning for him for about two days. Wank left the shack as the Keworgles guarded the pair. "Wait a minute.

We can transform ourselves into anything we want. I think this place is starting to rub off on us, we're not thinking clearly Pru," Winston said as if a light went on. "Wank disappears every day after breakfast and doesn't return until midafternoon. What can we transform into that would keep the Keworgles away?" Winston wondered out loud.

"I know," Pru replied with a grin on her face.

"What," he asked eagerly.

"Keworgles," silly she said, "Keworgles three times the size of Wank's two, that'll keep them away from us."

"Hey, good thinking, but can we do it?" Winston questioned.

"Just remember we need to have certainty," Pru reminded him.

"Easier said than done these days," he replied.

"You're letting doubts creep in. We need to meditate on the hieroglyphics on our medallions and ask for help, remember," she said removing her medallion hidden beneath her shirt.

Winston followed removing his medallion.

As they gazed into hieroglyphics engraved in the emerald and meditated, they began sensing these comforting, positive thoughts in their heads reminding them that they can do it…just have certainty. "You can't have certainty and create miracles if you allow fear and doubt to creep in," they heard in their minds. "You need to be aware of the fear and doubt to get rid of it." Remembering back on Luminatia they had such great certainty they were able to manifest anything in class with Myadora. After meditating for a long while, they each felt calm, relaxed and filled with confidence.

"What do you think? Pru asked.

"I feel great. Let's go for it," he said firmly with conviction.

It happened. Winston and Pru transformed into two huge Keworgles standing in front of the smaller ones now cowering at them in fear.

"Let's get out of here," Winston communicated with Pru telepathically.

Not sure how long the inexperienced transformers were going to be able to keep up this illusion; they raced out of the shack towards the road and ran for what seemed like miles. They found a cave off the road hidden behind some large rocks. There they transformed themselves back to normal.

"I think we'll be safe here for a while," Winston said as they sat in the cave catching their breath.

"How are we going to locate Godfrey?" Pru wanted to know.

"I'm not sure yet," he replied "Pru, do you sometimes hear something kinda like a soft voice in your head, but it's not really a voice more like an impression or an intuition?" he asked inquisitively.

"Yeah, I know what you're talking about. It's not really voices I almost feels like someone's trying to communicate with us maybe telepathically. It began when we met Wank and those scary Keworgles things. Who do you think could it be?" she asked with a scrunched up curious look on her face.

"I don't know," he said looking just as puzzled as Pru. "Maybe it has something to do with this guardian stuff."

"Ummm, ok, maybe. Ok that's what it's gotta be, it's the guardian stuff," she said with almost a sigh of relief. "Now what?"

"I think we should say here till morning, just in case Wank is out looking for us. This place feels safe and it's well hidden. In the meantime, let's eat, I'm hungry," he said digging into his shoulder sack, which was brimming over with nut butter, seeds, dried fruits and crackers.

"It's a good thing we remembered to bring food with us or we'd probably starve here," Pru quipped as she opened her shoulder sack. "The stuff Wank gave us to eat was despicable. It was like tasteless mud mush."

In the morning Pru turned to Winston, "Now what, where do we go?" she asked.

"First of all, wherever we go we need to be really careful. I'd don't know if there are more creepy people out there like Wank or what. If we have to, we can transform ourselves in an emergency but not in front of anyone. The thing is, you know we're not strong enough to keep it up for long periods of time. So, we really need to be aware of what's around us and keep on the lookout for safe places to duck into. We're gonna have to try to blend in. Most important is to stay focused," he instructed. "Ok! Let's do it."

Once outside the cave they climbed over the rocks back to the road. To the right the road led back towards Wank's shack, they went left. The road appeared to be in a rural area. Decaying trees and half dead bramble bushes covered the roadside. Hugging the side of the road the pair walked cautiously and silently for hours without seeing anyone, ready to jump into the bushes, if necessary, to hide.

"There's a fork in the road up ahead," Pru whispered.

"I see it," Winston replied.

"Which way, what do you think," Pru wanted to know.

"I have an idea, let's go behind the tree over there where no one can see us, we can use our medallions to meditate and see if it helps," Winston suggested.

"Brilliant!" Pru quipped. "You're beginning to think like a guardian."

After nearly an hour Winston turned to Pru, "Anything?"

"I'm not sure, I get a feeling we need to take the left fork," she replied.

"Hum! Interesting, me too, let's go," he directed.

Carefully as they made their way down another desolate road, eerie sounds emanated all around them, screeching, whistling, howling, cackling, sounds that were unrecognizable to their young ears.

Darkness began to set in and the two exhausted and unnerved from their day's ordeal, decide to look for some sort of cover. They found a large cluster of bushes surrounded by several trees and decided this was as good a place as any and collapsed on the ground.

"I'm so hungry," Pru confessed to Winston. "Winston, I'm scared and tired, I don't like this place. I've never been scared like this before."

"I know," he agreed as he removed some nuts and dried berries from his shoulder sack. "Me too! We just have to keep reminding ourselves there's a force on Egoshen that's trying to play with our minds. Remember what we learned about the veils of illusions. We have to focus on why we came here, to save Godfrey and bring him home. We need to have certainty, big time."

"Yeah, I know, but it's a whole lot easier to have certainty back home without all this scary stuff," she admitted as she finished her food then lied down on the ground using her shoulder sack as a pillow. I'm too tired. I'll deal with certainty tomorrow. Good night, Winston. I'm glad you're with me."

"Goodnight, Pru, I'm glad you're here with me too," he said lying down near her.

CHAPTER TWENTY-ONE

Startled awake from a deep sleep by the sounds of people screaming and yelling Winston and Pru quickly sat up confounded by the sudden inexplicable chaos this morning. "What's that, what's going on?" Pru said in an alarmed whisper.

"Don't know," Winston answers in a low voice as he crawled towards the bushes and peered through to see. "There's a man, a woman and a young boy. The man's shouting at the woman, waving his fist at her and the boy is crying.

Pru quietly moved next to Winston, observing the uproar unfolding in front of them. The tall stocky balding man in a rumpled grey jacket bellowed, "He's no son of mine, he shoulda' smacked that kid."

"Yeah Joey that's all you know, how to smack people. You're nothing but a big bully and I don't want my son growing up to be like you," replied the tired looking woman in a drab brown dress as she grabbed her son's hand and pulled him down the road. The man followed mumbling and shaking his fists in the air.

"Yikes!" Pru exclaimed. "What was that?"

"WOW! Chaos I suppose," Winston responded uneasy at the sight he just observed. "Myadora said that this place was full of chaos and I guess we just witnessed some."

"People don't act like that in Luminatia. These poor people I wish there was something we could do to help them all. What a terrible way to live your life," Pru sighed.

After eating breakfast, they set off on their journey to find Godfrey. The pair by this time looking somewhat disheveled from their ordeal, seemed to fit in with the surroundings, probably looking more like Egoshens.

As they walked down the road in the damp morning air, they noticed some small wooden houses scattered about the landscape. Trying to appear very much as they belonged, Winston and Pru came across a small village. Dismal looking houses were clustered together in rows surrounding what appeared to be the main street, which was crammed with a variety of bleak shops. Tottering in and out of the shops and up and down the street were very dreary, sullen looking inhabitants.

"Winston! Pru!" a voice called from behind.

Stunned, the two turned to see a slight, frail man with white curly hair and thick rimless glasses.

"Who are you?" Winston demanded.

"It's ok, my friends. Don't be fearful, I'm Garren. Myadora told me to expect you," the man said lowering his glasses slightly revealing his twinkling blue eyes. "Come with me, we can't talk here."

Hearing Myadora's name, the two young guardians breathed a sigh of relief. They smiled then silently followed Garren through the bleak streets laden with old dirty crushed cans, broken bottles, crumpled papers, rotten foodstuffs and a variety of disgusting unidentifiable garbage. The trio walked rapidly through the village filled with unwelcoming, cheerless houses. There were broken windows boarded up with wood or cardboard. Rickety fences with peeling paint bordered some of the houses and a variety of discarded objects were dumped around the front yards.

At the edge of the village they came upon a dirt road. "It's this way my young friends," Garren guided them in a soothing reassuring voice.

There were fewer houses off this road. Continuing in silence they walked about another two miles. "We're almost there, just up this path," the frail little man announced as he pointed towards the direction of his home.

A small light blue house with white trim was now visible through the bushes. "Here now, come in. It's safe here, we can talk," he assured Winston and Pru. "But first, let's get you cleaned up and some food."

Inside the tidy house there appeared to be three rooms. The larger room was a combination kitchen, living room. A plain wooden table surrounded by four matching chairs stood in the kitchen area. There was a pair of overstuffed, high-backed, olive-green tweed wing chairs flanking the fireplace. The comfortable sofa was positioned across from the chairs. In the second room, a neatly kept bedroom, a blue and brown patchwork quilt covered a double bed. A twin sized bed and table with a lamp occupied the tiny third room.

"Why don't the two of you get cleaned up, while I prepare some dinner? We'll talk later, I'm sure you have lots of questions," Garren acknowledged.

"Thank you, that sounds great," Winston sighed wearily.

"Yes, thank you," Pru chimed in as they both took turns cleaning up.

The table was filled with meat, mashed potatoes with gravy, an assortment of cooked vegetables and freshly baked bread.

"Wow!" Pru exclaimed. "How did you get all this done so fast?"

Garren smiled and winked.

"Who are you?" Winston curiously inquired.

"Like you, I'm a guardian," Garren said removing his medallion from beneath his shirt, showing it to Pru and Winston. "I was sent here a very, very long time ago from the "Kingdom of Lights" to aid people in Egoshen. I'm sure you noticed from your journey Candiff, which by the way is the name of this village, is not a very happy place. People here like in all parts of Egoshen live in chaos. As you'll observe while you're in Egoshen people are almost always in some state of dread. They desire a better life but don't believe they deserve it.

Unlike Egoshen, the people in Luminatia have just enough challenges and pain in their lives so when they work through them; they are able to appreciate the joy. Luminations, as you know, are taught early in life what to do to conquer their challenges. They understand that their challenges are there to help them become better people and live good lives.

But when Egoshens have a challenge, they react by getting angry and resentful. They do nothing about overcoming their challenges. People here have just enough joy so they don't realize how much pain, unhappiness and chaos they really have in their lives."

"Myadora taught us about the veils of illusions and what it does to people's minds," Winston acknowledged.

"Being here you'll witness it firsthand. People delude themselves believing they know what love is but they don't have a clue. Although Avadon has already placed veils of illusions on these people, to feed his power he continues to play with their minds. He reinforces these illusions so they're unable to remember even the slightest detail of their wonderful lives in Luminatia. The longer these people remain in Egoshen the more veils they acquire," Garren explained. "If you think of a lighted lamp and you put a veil over it. One is still able to see a little through the veil. But if you keep putting more veils over that lamp, eventually all you see is darkness and it becomes harder to get through those veils and back to the light. That's what Avadon does with these veils to people's minds."

"In order to help these people our teachings begin by example. Some become curious about the different way we are living. When we find an opening with those who are amenable, we go on to use other methods in order to assist them in removing the veils. We help them learn to live by the principle Luminations live by which is "to treat others with love, kindness and respect the way they themselves would want to be treated. We have had successes, but it's a long hard road. Enough shop talk as we say. Did you have enough to eat?" Garren asked.

"Yes, thank you," Pru answered politely.

"How does Myadora know we're here?" Winston finally asked seeming puzzled by Garren's revelation.

"To put it simply, she is an old and very experienced guardian with heightened senses and abilities. She is able tune into both of you wherever you might be," Garren explained.

"Do you think she's mad at us?" Pru wanted to know.

"No, she understands, but is concerned," he replied.

"You're both exhausted. Get some sleep and we'll talk more in the morning. Winston why don't you take the larger bedroom and Pru take the smaller one. Sleep well. My young guardian."

"Thanks," Winston wearily said. "But where are you going to sleep?"

"The sofa will do me fine," replied Garren.

Both Winston and Pru dragged themselves to their respective bedrooms. They fell into bed and into a very deep sleep.

CHAPTER TWENTY-TWO

After an early breakfast and finishing his morning meditation, Garren settled himself into the chair near the fireplace. His attention focused on Winston and Pru anxiously seated on the sofa across from him bursting with questions.

"I know you must have lots of questions for me, you've been very patient," Garren said. "Meditation in one of the ways I'm able to connect with others from the Kingdom of Lights. In this negative environment it helps to keep me grounded. I recommend you do the same. It will aid you in keeping your minds clear. It's difficult living in these negative circumstances is very easy to get caught up in this destructive atmosphere. It's so important to constantly be on guard."

"Candiff is just one small village in Egoshen," Garren continued. "There are many other villages, towns as well as big cities. Manfreed von Neever, the so-called King or Ruler of Egoshen is really Avadon and Queen Feendra, is his sister Angeen. They've transformed themselves believing people of Egoshen won't recognize their evil.

You need to be extremely careful should you meet or come into the sight of those two they will identify you as being from Luminatia. You must create an illusion of having the demeanor of an Egoshen. A mudwonk needs to be attached to your left ear. Avadon and certain of his loyal allies who have been given the authority and who roam the streets are the only ones who are able see the mudwonks and as guardians you don't have a mudwonk. To everyone else they are invisible," Garren, advised.

"What is a mudwonk?' Winston asked wondering what's next.

"When a person arrives in Egoshen a mudwonk is assigned to them. This creature will stay with them for their entire life for the sole purpose of watching over and assisting in creating more chaos in the life of their assignee. Due to the fact each person is living in an illusion and all though the mudwonk never leaves their side, the people are unable see or have knowledge of it." Garren went on.

"Mudwonks stand about three feet high with dark brown glistening flaccid matted fur coats. When erect you're unable to discern where their head, arms or legs are…they resemble a mound of bloated, sagging mud. Their eyeballs dangle out of very flabby sockets drooping down to their midsection …their mouth resembles a thick hose with lips at the end. Due to their short stature, they have the ability to elongate their hose like mouths in order to reach and attach it to their assignee's ear. Their dangling eyes have the capability to extend up or around for the purpose of observation in all directions," Garren explained.

"Ugg, what else are we going to find in this foul place?" Pru said feeling disgusted. "Garren, do you know where we can find Godfrey?" Pru asked.

"No dear Pru," he replied. "If you and Winston are to find your brother, you will both somehow be guided to him. But if you are not to find him you might be guided wrongly. Remember and this is very important, when the time comes for you to return home, which is two hours before the next new moon in Luminatia, you both must absolutely go back to the cave immediately. Make your way to the secret window with or without Godfrey. There are drastic consequences for not getting back on time. You will be trapped in Egoshen. Your knowledge and powers as a guardian will cease to exist and therefore you will have to live as an Egoshen. Finally, you never be able to help or see Godfrey. If in fact you do return to the secret window on time without finding Godfrey, you may have another opportunity in the future to return to Egoshen to find him. Do you both understand what could be a catastrophic outcome if you don't heed my warnings and advise? Please give me your solemn word you will abide by this or I cannot help you go on."

"Yes," said Winston with conviction.

Pru echoed, "Yes, certainly. But since time in Egoshen is different than Luminatia, how will we know when we need to return?"

"Guardians from the Kingdom of Light will guide you when the time is right. For now, I'll bring you to the road at the edge of the village it will lead you on to where you need to go. Remember, listen, use your intuition and you will be guided. Take great care not to be recognized and don't travel after dark," Garren counseled the two.

Filling their shoulder sacks with food and water Garren related to them, "There is a city about thirty miles down the road. I've got two bicycles you can use which will get you their quickly. Do not bring them into the city it will be dangerous. Leave them chained to the red post just outside of the city. They will be returned to me."

"Thank you for all your help and we will listen to your advice." Winston insisted gratefully.

"Yes, thank you so much," Pru reiterated.

CHAPTER TWENTY-THREE

The road was just a short distance from Garren's house. Saying goodbye to their new friend the pair began to cycle single file, Winston leading Pru following him down the road towards the city of Mulduchin. Along the way the scenery improved. Pine trees line the road and the foul odors they encountered upon their arrival in Egoshen have been replaced by the scent of pine.

After traveling about eight or nine miles they noticed several well-kept houses on the hillside and cars which were unfamiliar to Luminatia began to appear on the road. There were cars transporting what appeared to be families, others just individuals. Some of the cars were shiny and new. It was a big change from the shabbiness of the earlier sights.

Winston signaled to Pru to pull off the road. There ahead was a small, secluded area. "This looks like a good place to rest up for a while and eat. I'm starving." Winston said.

"You're always starving," she laughed as they hid the bicycles behind some bushes and ate lunch.

They reach the red post just outside Mulduchin about three in the afternoon. As they chained the bicycles up to the post, Pru turned to Winston, "I'm sooo tired. My legs ache, my bottom is sore and I'm not getting any intuitions. What now… are you getting anything?"

"No, we've been on those bikes for nearly four hours. I think our brains have fogged up. Let's just find a place to rest for a little while," Winston said as the two began to scout about for a safe place.

"Look over there," Pru said pointing to a broken-down vacant shack with empty cardboard boxes, newspapers and cans strewn about. "What about there?"

"I guess it looks ok," Winston replied heading for the shack. "I don't think we should go inside, just in case someone comes. We'll be safer outside, but we need to stay out of sight. Look there's big box over there, let's check it out."

Weary from their day's travels the young guardians sat down inside the large cardboard box not feeling much like guardians at the moment. They did not intend to fall asleep, but sleep they did.

"Who are you two?" a voice shouted from outside the cardboard box.

Startled awake, Winston and Pru stared at the figure of a young teenage boy with spiked red and blue hair standing outside the box with his hands on his hips. "I said who you are?" the boy repeated in a very threatening manner.

"I'm, Wi," Winston started to say. "I'm Will and this is my sister," he hesitated, "Jill."

"Will and Jill, isn't that cute, do you have another brother named Phil or a sister named Lil?" the boy responded sarcastically. "You're in my house get out of there and maybe I need to hurt you." the boy mumbled angrily, as two more boys appeared behind him in the dim light of early evening.

"What do we do?" Pru asked Winston telepathically.

Answering in the same way, Winston said, "Well, first we've got to hold it together and I guess, as you always put it, we need to use our guardian stuff. I think it might be time for Phil and Lil to appear. If we really concentrate and stay calm, I believe we can create an illusion of being in two places at the same time. We stay in the box as ourselves and create the illusion of our very big brother Phil and our very big sister Lil, outside in back of these guys. We need to focus with certainty."

"Hi guys, having a problem with our little brother and sister, Will and Jill?" a very husky voice bellowed from behind the three boys. As the three turned they caught sight of a huge, six-foot six-inch man with a scruffy beard. "Heard you were looking for me, I'm Phil. Oh yeah, by the way this is my sister Lil," he said pointing to the equally huge, six-foot two inch, bulked up woman next to him.

The three bullies cowered, frozen in place their mouths hung open, as they stared at the figures who seemed to appear out of nowhere, "Nope, uh, uh, no problem," the first boy said beginning to stutter. "Nnnnn no, no problem, we were just messing around." As Phil and Lil came closer the three boys turned and darted off into the night.

Winston and Pru smiled at each other with a great sense of relief. "I think it might be a good idea if we kept our big brother and sister with us for a bit longer. We can probably keep the illusion going for a little while hopefully until we find a safe place. What do you think?" Winston asked.

"Ok! Let's go for it. I'm really glad we did our homework and a lot of practicing transformations when we were back in Luminatia," Pru said with a sigh of relief.

It was dark and the lights of Mulduchin shown brightly in the distance as the illusion of four made their way carefully towards the city.

Pru and Winston could hear Garren's warning in their heads and they knew no matter how difficult it was they had to keep up the illusion of Phil and Lil. At least with the adults they had manifested accompanying them, they would be safe for a little while.

When they reached the outskirts of the city, they realized they needed find a safe place to spend the night. As they ventured further into the city, the streets were overflowing with people hurrying about. There were elegant stores and restaurants, streets with large apartment houses and office buildings.

Trying to blend in with their surroundings was becoming difficult for Winston and Pru and their rather large illusions.

The extreme height of their creations was drawing stares from passersby and keeping up the illusion of Phi and Lil became a more arduous task. It had been more than two hours since they had created the illusionary adults. The uncertainty of being alone in this foreign city after dark with all of these strangers about was beginning to unnerve the two young guardians. Without having complete certainty their powers were starting to diminish.

They felt an urgent need to do something, but the stress of their situation was affecting their abilities and their intuition. Weaving in and around the people in the crowded brightly lit streets they looked for a safe place for the night. But where, everything was well lit they there did not seem to be any out of the way place to take cover for the night.

Without warning Phil and Lil disappeared. Hoping no one had noticed the sudden disappearance; Winston and Pru were now completely alone. "Whatta we gonna do?" Winston nervously asked Pru.

"I don't know," Pru answered as her eyes begin to fill with tears. "Maybe everyone was right in Luminatia, maybe we shouldn't have come here. We're just kids, whatta we know anyhow? Winston I'm scared, I can feel the negativity of this place creeping into my mind and trying to take over," said the eleven-year old guardian.

Trying to appear confident Winston attempted to put his friend's mind at ease, "Don't worry Pru, we'll find someplace. It'll be ok, really. Pru we're guardians, we can do this. We're gonna figure it out," he said with great optimism in his voice. Not really believing a word he was saying, but making an effort to calm and reassure Pru and perhaps convenience himself.

They could feel the stares of the people clopping down the street, looking at two children out alone at night. Hearts beating rapidly in their chests fearing someone would reveal their true identities to the authorities so that they could never return home, Winston and Pru continued to search for someplace to hide for the night.

As they approached the corner of the next street the two sighted a fairly large park covering several blocks. Quickly and carefully crossing the street towards the park, they could still feel eyes watching them. They saw some brightly lit paths, but also a lot of dark brush covered areas as well. Ducking into some of the brush and keeping clear of the lit paths, Winston guided Pru deeper in to park. Clouds filled the night sky hiding the light of the moon making it difficult for them to maneuver. Feeling their way up some shadowy hills, past clumps of trees and bushes, they anxiously explored the area looking for a safe place. Noises in the darkness unnerved the two as they remembered some of the creatures they had seen earlier in their journey. What other kind of weird creatures could this place produce? Clouds above seemed to part and the faint light of the moon revealed a hillside covered with large boulders and bushes. "Look," Winston said pointing to the boulder, "there's gotta be a place up there that's safe, don't you think?"

Pru agreed.

Carefully they climbed the hill. There was a wide crevice between two of the boulders and they decided this would be a safe place to spend the night. After having something to eat and resting for a while, the two began to feel a little less anxious.

"Oh Winston, I'm really scared. What are we going to do?" said Pru hesitantly, while leaning back against the boulder with her chin in her hands.

"Pru, I keep telling you we're gonna be ok. I know it. We just need some sleep, things will look different in the morning," Winston replied struggling to appear confident for her sake, while at the same time thinking he never wanted to come to this place and he definitely was not sure he wanted to be a guardian. After all he was just a twelve-year old kid, not some superhero. But there was Pru, looking so frightened, trembling and trying to look brave. He suddenly began to feel very protective of her and knew he needed to get rid of his doubts fast. Not so long ago he remembered telling Willow he wanted to be an adventurer or an explorer when he got older. "If this is an adventure, be careful what you wish for," he thought.

Unexpectedly their golden medallions seemed to leap from beneath their shirts. An amazing green energy emanated from the radiant emeralds set in the center of the medallions. The green light shot into their eyes and began to envelop their bodies practically mesmerizing them. As they continued to stare, they could make out some letterings appearing in the stones. Calmness began to replace their feelings of fear and uncertainty.

A twinkling light began to swirl around Winston and Pru. "Hello my young guardians," Myadora said as she appeared in the same green light surrounding her charges.

"Myadora," they exclaimed looking stunned at the transparent vision before them.

"What are you doing here? Winston asked.

"I'm here to warn you my dear ones. The evil power of Avadon is everywhere and the same negative energy force he uses on the people of Egoshen will affect you as well. It will begin to play with your minds and I believe it already has to some small degree. Negativity is infectious unless you protect yourself from it. You must always remember the light force is with you and within you. It's essential that you use it. Egoshen will be extremely dangerous to you if you forget this," Myadora cautioned the two youngsters sitting nervously in front of her. "Your powers will diminish if you allow this negativity and fear to take over. You must constantly be aware."

"It's hard not to be afraid here," Pru fretted.

"I know my sweet," Myadora answered sympathetically. "But what are you afraid of? You've forgotten this is all part of an illusion created by Avadon. Pru, illusions are not real, unless you buy into and believe in them. Only then do they do seem real."

"So, what you saying is, just having certainty the light force is within us. And by remembering this is all an illusion, not real, will keep us from being afraid and we will be able to use our powers," Winston responded.

"Yes, just trust in the power of the positive energy force," Myadora said. "It's that simple and yet very difficult at the same time.

"Why difficult?" Pru asked.

"Because Avadon is very clever and will try to trick you into believing things are real. Be strong my dear ones, you've chosen this journey. There is a great guardian here in Egoshen, Valeness. You will meet him in your travels. Sleep now, you have a difficult journey ahead. I have confidence in the two of you," Myadora said as her image disappeared.

That meant a lot to Winston and Pru. They were exhausted and fell asleep quickly.

CHAPTER TWENTY-FOUR

The following morning loud chattering in the park woke them. They peered out over one of the boulders that kept them hidden to see several people scurrying about on a large platform. A crowd was beginning to gather around the platform as a group of musicians seated nearby began to practice. The two decided that it would be safer for the present to remain hidden. The bushes near one of the boulders gave them cover and allowed them to view the activities below.

The crowd grew larger until the entire field below was covered. A motorcade of cars and motorbikes with sirens blasting drove through a path nearby and stopped at the side of the platform. Emerging from the cars were several dozen uniformed men carrying large weapons. They encircled the massive gold car in the middle of the motorcade.

Six men in white suits appeared from within the gold car followed by a beautiful, slender woman. Her straight long black hair was pulled back off her face. She wore a plain tailored white dress accented with gold jewelry. Last to leave the car dressed in an elegant white uniform trimmed in gold braids was a handsome tall man with black hair and a long, pointed nose. He stood about six inches taller than the woman. The crowd cheered; the noise was deafening. Cheers turned into chants, "Manfreed! Manfreed! Manfreed!"

The guards surrounded the couple and led them to the platform.

A chill ran up their spines when Winston and Pru realized they were actually looking at Avadon and Angeen who had transformed themselves into the rulers of Egoshen. They sat transfixed staring through the bushes as the so-called, King Manfreed von Neever and his sister, Queen Feendra climbed up to the platform. As the king neared the podium he seemed to look over in the direction of Winston and Pru.

It was not fear that the two young guardians felt. It was absolute terror. Could he see them? Did he know they were there? With their hearts pounding in their chests, they stood frozen and hardly took a breath.

King Manfreed began to speak to the crowd. His memorizing gaze hypnotized the multitude of people before him, who were intensely listening to his every word. He could have told them yellow elephants were flying above and purple pigs were dancing in the streets. They would have believed him. It did not matter what he said or did, they all blindly bought into his illusions and lies.

He had a cunning smile, as he looked down his long nose at his subjects. Announcing to them how lucky they were to have a king that cared so much for his people and wanted so much for them. He lied with such ease. Informing them of all the new improvements he was preparing for them. But of course, these beneficial improvements would be rather expensive. Naturally their taxes had to once again be raised for all the benefits they believed they were about to receive but in reality, these improvements would never happen. The people were deceived into trusting that he has their best interests at heart and cheered at his every word. His illusion was perfect.

Manfreed ruled by fear and intimidation, while appearing to be concerned and considerate towards his people. When it served his own purposes, he permitted some of his subjects to have great wealth but not happiness, at the same time a great deal lived in absolute poverty. There are those who are somewhere in the middle. They have some monetary comfort but are always dissatisfied and desire more. He allowed the people to believe they were in control of their lives, when in fact he has complete control and keeps them living in chaos.

"Do you think he knows we're here? He keeps looking in this direction," Pru asked Winston with great concern, forgetting everything Myadora recently said.

"I don't know," he answered. "But I don't think we should hang around here to find out. Pru you're allowing yourself to get caught up in his illusion. Remember what Myadora said."

"You're right. But how do we get out of here without being seen?" Pru questioned, looking at the boulders in front of them and the path they used the night before. "If we try to leave someone is going to see us. There's no way."

"Yep! I think there is," Winston told Pru with a smile. "Just remember what Myadora said about our powers. If we let fear in, our powers diminish. Well, if we don't let fear in, we've got powers, right."

"Right," Pru said looking puzzled. "What are you thinking?"

"What can climb quickly over the boulders, look natural in this setting and get us away from Avadon and the crowds?" he asked.

"I don't know. What?" Pru asked.

"Squirrels," he said with a big grin on his face.

"Squirrels!" Pru exclaimed.

"Yeah," Winston said. "They're small. They're fast and can get over the boulders without being noticed. No one will pay any attention to a squirrel," he said with a new air of confidence.

"Expect by Manfreed, I mean Avadon," she said defiantly.

"Ok!" he thought out loud and then said, "but only by Avadon. So, we have to transform and wait until he's looking in another direction and then run up across the back boulders. We need to do it very quickly. There's no other choice. If we stay here, we're probably going to get caught, it's our only chance. We can do it, Pru. Remember no fear. Are you ready?"

Pru smiled at him, "Yeah, let's go for it."

The two put on their shoulder sacks and sat on the ground. They started to concentrate on transforming themselves into squirrels. It took them several minutes until they were able to make the transformation. Winston watched Avadon through the bushes near the boulders. Avadon kept glancing over to where the two squirrels were ready to make their escape.

It looked as though they were not going to be able to leave and were not sure how long they could keep the illusion of being squirrels. They had to remain calm and focused. If they allowed fear in, they were definitely in trouble. Twenty minutes passed, as Avadon seemed to be transfixed on their location.

Suddenly, there was a loud, "POP, POP," sound that came from the crowd, followed by what seemed to be some kind of fireworks. Avadon's attention turned towards they commotion in the crowd.

"Let's go now," Winston cried.

CHAPTER TWENTY-FIVE

The two squirrels raced across the boulders and out of sight. They continued to run through the park until they reached the street. "Let's keep going," Pru commanded telepathically as they ran into the street.

"I think we need to keep the squirrel illusion going for a while. It'll be safer," Winston suggested.

"I agree," Pru, responded as the pair of squirrels ran quickly along the streets of Mulduchin. Unsure of where they were heading, they knew they had to put as much distance between themselves and Avadon as possible.

After running through Mulduchin for several hours, Winston suggested to Pru, "There's a large tree up ahead. As squirrels we could climb up onto a high branch and rest for a while. At least up there we'll be safe."

"You know I like climbing trees," Pru reminded him. "I've just never done it as a squirrel."

The rough bark of the tree made it a little difficult for the inexperienced squirrel climbers. At one point, Winston was unable to get his claws to dig into the bark and began to slip. Remarkably he regained his footing and continued up the tree.

As they sat high enough in the treetop not to be observed from below, they transformed back to themselves. Reminiscing about the day's events feeling more confident, grateful they were safely able to get past Avadon, Pru said, "Myadora was right this place is filled with illusions and if we're careful, focused, use our abilities as guardians and keep remembering there's nothing to be afraid of, we'll be ok."

"We should stay transformed as squirrels. I'm not sure where we need to go. I know it should at least be in the opposite direction of where we saw Avadon, I mean Manfreed von Neever," he quipped.

The houses in the area were well kept. Trees and shrubbery were plentiful so if necessary, they could duck and hide. Being a squirrel, this was fun. They could run fast, climb trees, jump from branch to branch scurry under bushes. "What an adventure," Winston thought pleased at the experience.

A little further down the street, they noticed a little boy of about six years old, standing and watching them. As they ran past him, he began to hurl rocks at them.

"Ouch," said Pru, as one of the rocks hit her in the head.

"Are you ok?" Winston communicated telepathically, as the two continued to run.

"Yeah, let's get away from this kid, fast," she replied as they headed towards the end of the block and into the street. The little boy continued running right behind them tossing more rocks.

Apparently, it appeared as though the young boy might not have been permitted to cross the street. When he reached the curb, he stopped. They ran for few more blocks until the boy was out of sight and then they climbed up into a tree. Winston checked Pru's face. She had suffered a small bruise on her right cheek and was fine.

"We'd better get going," Winston said as the two climbed down and began running along grass near the curb.

It was Pru who first spotted what looked to be an empty schoolyard about a block away. "I'll race you," she said as she ran towards the street, about twenty feet in front of Winston.

"You may be ahead of me, but I'll catch you and beat you to the big tree in the school yard," he said gaining on her.

As Pru ran across the street a large blue car raced down the same street. Pru did not see the car, but Winston did. The car was about to run over Pru. She saw it but it was too late, the car sped over her. In that instant frozen with fear he was no longer a squirrel. He tried to shout but there was not enough time.

Sitting near the curb in a state of shock with his eyes closed and his body trembling, he heard a voice.

"Winston."

He opened his eyes and sitting the middle of the street was Pru, her body trembling.

"Pru, Pru, you're not, not dead," he stuttered running towards her. "What happened?"

"I don't know," she said as tears filled her eyes. "I saw the car and I couldn't run, I just froze, I guess because I was a small squirrel, I wasn't hit, the car just went right over me."

"What just happened, how did you do that?" asked the puzzled and dazed young eleven-year old boy who had been playing behind the tree in the schoolyard and witnessed the whole thing. "I saw the car was gonna hit a squirrel and then you both came out of nowhere. You were squirrels," he could not believe what he just saw.

"What do you mean what happened," Winston said regaining his composure while attempting to quickly come up with a plausible explanation. "My, my sister almost got hit by a car. I saw a squirrel running in front of her. She may have been watching it and probably didn't see the car and then she rolled out of the way of the car."

"Uh-uh, nope, that's not what happened, I saw the whole thing. You were squirrels and then you weren't," the young boy insisted defiantly as he stared at Pru still sitting in the street.

Winston helped Pru to her feet. She was not hurt, just shaken up. He led her to the curb while trying very hard to ignore the boy. It was not working the boy was adamant about what he saw. Winston decided to try another approach.

"I know what you think you saw," Winston said trying to appear confused. "But how can squirrels become people or people become squirrels, that's ridiculous. It's impossible? You must have a really good imagination. My name is Will and this is my sister Jill," Winston said trying to change the subject. "Who are you?"

"I'm Arnie," the boy announced, still not convinced about Winston's answer but not knowing what else to say and maybe feeling a little doubtful. "Do you live around here?"

"No, were visiting our aunt," Pru said as she stood up and brushed herself off. "We've gotta go. Come on Will."

"Hey, can I walk with you for a little while?" Arnie asked.

"Don't you have to be someplace?" said Pru trying to sound rude.

"Nope!" Arnie replied.

"Sure Arnie," Winston said trying to appear blasé about the situation. He was not sure how to get rid of Arnie.

The three of them walked along the school grounds. Neither, Pru or Winston had any idea of where they were heading.

"What are we going to do?" Pru asked Winston telepathically as she glanced in Arnie's direction.

"I don't know. Let's just be casual," he answered her in the same way.

Arnie looked puzzled at his two new friends. "How are you two talking without moving your mouths and what don't you know and what are you being casual about?" he said repeating what he had just overheard.

Startled by Arnie's questions and revelation, Pru and Winston gasped and struggled to find an answer that he would understand or accept.

"Ok something weird is going on here. First, you're both squirrels, then become kids, then you try and make me think I'm seeing things and then you talk to each other and nothings comes out of your mouths," Arnie rambled apprehensively and perplexed with what he had been observing. "Who are you two? What are you two? Uh-Uh I'm not crazy. I know what I saw and I know what I heard. I'm gonna tell my father, he's on the City Council you know."

Winston burst out laughing, "Ok Pru, lets tell him the truth.

Not having a clue what he was talking about, she replied, "Sure, the truth, yep tell him the truth."

"Would you believe we've come from another dimension to find Pru's brother who was kidnapped by an evil wizard and brought here?"

"No," Arnie said. "You really think I'm that dumb?"

"Would you believe we've been practicing to be magicians? You know, like illusionists and we've been throwing our voices like ventriloquists so we don't move our mouths." Winston said with a smile on his face.

"I knew it had to be something like that. Wow can you show me some more tricks," Arnie said relieved he had finally gotten to the truth.

Pru and Winston smiled at each other and knew they could not communicate telepathically in front of Arnie.

Winston created a few illusions of pulling different object out of Arnie's pockets, which seemed to please his new friend. Pru's illusion had voices coming from Arnie's shoes. They tried to keep the illusions simple in hopes that Arnie would be satisfied with their explanation and not alarmed by their actions.

Arnie seemed fascinated and amused by their so-called magic tricks and being a very curious eleven-year old, wanted to know how they were done. Winston advised him about the magician's code of not being able to reveal the secrets to performing the tricks.

Sensing Arnie's satisfaction with the answers and performances he had just witnessed, Winston thought it might a safe time to leave. He was curious, though about Arnie's ability to hear their telepathic conversations. It was too dangerous to mention, it could raise red flags and let the young boy know there was really something different about his two new friends.

"Well, Arnie," Winston said motioning to Pru. "We had fun and I'm glad you liked our magic tricks, but we've gotta get going, it's getting late. We'll see you around."

"Yep, you will," Arnie winked as he turned to walk away and begin to whistle.

Pru and Winston knew they could not communicate telepathically just yet, glanced at each other with puzzled looks on their faces. What did he mean, "Yep you will?"

Their encounter with Arnie left the two quite unnerved and they decided it would probably be a good idea not to communicate in any way for a while.

CHAPTER TWENTY-SIX

After walking more than an hour or so through the pristine upscale residential area of the city, the appearance of neighborhood began to change. Crossing the bridge over the cement riverbed the houses seemed to be smaller and closer together. A few were shabby and not well kept. There was however, quite an array of vibrant multi colored houses, some decorated with painted flowers others with colorful geometric shapes.

"I feel like I'm walking through one of my mother paintings," Winston remarked. Recalling how she would repeatedly say 'there's no such thing as too many colors in a painting, after all think of all the wonderful varieties of color you find in a garden.' He missed his mother and his sister. Children playing in front yards were dressed in vividly colored clothes.

"This place looks really amazing," Pru said. "But which way should we to go? There are lots of different streets and roads I don't know which one we're supposed to take. I'm not getting any kind of feeling, are you?

"Nothing. I guess we just keep walking until we do," he answered feeling a little disappointed.

"What do you make of that kid Arnie?" Pru asked. "I got a weird feeling the way he sounded so sure that he was going to see us again. Creepy! Huh?"

"Yeah! And how come he could hear us when we were talking telepathically, that was freaky. I'm just wondering if there's some way we could figure out more about him. Is he just a weird kid on the street or is he someone who could be dangerous to us? He said his father was on the City Council. I'm not sure if that means anything," Winston exclaimed with a bit of concern in his voice as they continued walking.

No one talked for a quite a while, there did not seem to be anything to say. They could not come up with any answers as to who or what Arnie was and decided they would deal with that question later.

The spring like air felt good. It helped to clear the cobwebs of all negativity surrounding their eventful morning from their minds. They walked quietly focusing their attention on nothing special, the sky, the birds and the flowers.

"I just got that real strong feeling we need to find a bright green house with big purple flowers in the front yard. It was like a vision I could see it in my mind. Winston, I don't know how, but I know it's here somewhere," Pru said with absolute confidence at the prospect of find another clue that might bring them closer to Godfrey's possible whereabouts.

"Huh! Me too. I know exactly what you're talking about. There's a very colorful windmill on top of the house," Winston replied with a curious look on his face recognizing something new was happening to them.

Not only was their intuition returning but also this was different there was more. The two of them actually saw the same thing in their mind's eye. "I have a feeling we may be getting another power," Pru said excited by the realization that something new was manifesting. "I think it's the power of seeing."

"WOW! This is amazing," he replied. "If we could see the house, maybe we could see Godfrey."

"Oh, I hope so," she said as her eyes filled with tears.

It was already late in the afternoon and the pair had been walking for most of the day. They needed to find a quiet place where they could concentrate and use their powers to help them find the green house. Up ahead was a commercial area with shops and restaurants. Once again, like the houses in this neighborhood these buildings were covered in brightly colored paint.

At the end of the street there was a square with a small park the center. Three streets led away from the square. On one corner sat a colorful play area filled with children. Adults talked together as the children climbed on, up and through a little obstacle course. A couple sat having a conversation in the gazebo in the center of the park. Benches were placed near the greenery and flowers grew in abundance throughout the park. Pru and Winston smiled.

"If I didn't know any better, I'd think we were in Luminatia. These people look and seem to act differently than anyone we've come across in Egoshen," Pru remarked.

"You're right, I wonder what's going on here," Winston agreed.

They walked over to one of the empty benches near a cluster of bushes and sat down. There were not many people nearby. Feeling safe now that they seemed able to blend in and no one was paying much attention to them, Winston and Pru sat quietly. Closing their eyes, they began to focus on getting some direction in finding the green house.

They sat in a meditative state for about twenty minutes, feeling totally relaxed and at peace. The answer came to them simultaneously, "We need to take the street to the right," they said in unison.

"Then go left when we see the donkey, look for a wishing well and follow the chimes. Wow that was amazing!" Pru said giggling. "I have no idea what this means."

"Me neither, but let's go," Winston said as he jumped up off the bench excited to get started. "It was so clear. I've never felt anything like that before, I got the same message."

About ten minutes passed as they headed down the street to the right of the square. There it was just as they had seen in their vision, right in front of them on the front lawn was a donkey. Well not a real donkey, it was a stuffed animal probably left there by some child, but nonetheless it was a donkey.

The young guardians felt energized, they knew with certainty that their visions were leading them in the right direction to the green house. Four blocks further down they saw written on the street sign, *Wishing Well Lane.* The green house had to be there somewhere, but where? The air was still. There were no sounds of chimes to be heard and there did not seem to be anything matching the description of the house they were trying to locate. A light breeze blew and there it was, the angelic sound of crystal glass wind chimes. Closing their eyes, the two tried to discern the direction of these angelic sounds.

"This way," Pru said as she pulled Winston by the hand.

There was no green house. The chimes seemed to come from a large blue house with purple shutters. "It's not green," said Winston looking a little disappointed.

Pru stood in front of the blue house for a moment with her eyes closed and said with delight, "It's coming from the back."

The two ran up the long driveway towards the back of the house past some tall bushes and stopped dead in their tracks. There it was the green house with a row of purple hydrangea bushes on each side of the front door and on the roof was the multi-colored windmill.

Looking at each other, Pru whispered to Winston, "What do we do now?"

He stared at the house and then focused his eyes on Pru and smiled, "I guess we knock."

"Knock," she echoed.

"Yeah, I don't think we were guided here just to stare at the house," said Winston as he took Pru's hand and led her to the lavender front door. Squeezing her hand, he put his finger on the doorbell and pressed.

The sound of the crystal wind chimes seemed to get louder as they stood frozen to the spot not knowing who or what was going to open the door.

CHAPTER TWENTY-SEVEN

"I've been expecting you," Safaira said as she led them into the green house.

"You have," Winston said cautiously.

The house was cheerful with lots of colors and prints decorating the interior. Would you like some lemonade?" she asked smiling at the two children as she showed them into the kitchen.

"Yes please, that would be nice," they answered not understanding why they felt so comfortable in her presence.

A few minutes later Safaira brought two glasses of lemonade and some sandwiches for them. She sat quietly across the table from them as they ate their sandwiches and drank their lemonade. When they finished, she invited them into the living room. They sat on the beautifully colored floral sofa while she sat on the lavender chair across from them. It felt like déjà vu, it was like being back with Garren.

"I'm Safaira," she said gently. "Like you, I'm a guardian, but I've been here on Egoshen for many lifetimes."

"Can't you go home to Luminatia?" Pru asked concerned for Safaira. "And if you've been here lifetimes why don't you look older?"

"Of course, I can go back," she replied, "but I choose to stay. There are so many people here who need my help. As to not looking older, time here in Egoshen is different. If you were to measure it against time in Luminatia, an hour there might be equivalent to a year in Egoshen. Guardians in Egoshen are able to see other guardians in the same way they would appear in Luminatia. Guardians who remain in Egoshen have the ability to appear the way people in this world need to see them."

"Do Winston and I appear older to the Egoshens?" Pru asked.

"No. You haven't been here long enough," she answered.

"This place is different than any of the other places we've seen so far in Egoshen. Most of the houses are so colorful. It was like walking through a painting," Winston commented as he noticed an easel standing near a large bay window in the alcove off to the right of the living room.

"I love color and love to paint," Safaira related to her guests. "Painting also helps a lot of the people I work with. Calenda was once a very dreary and sad looking little town. Most of the people here didn't have very much. When I arrived in this small community, I could feel the downheartedness of its residents. One of my powers is to be able to understand and sense how people feel. Most endured hardships. They were preoccupied with their own needs and desires."

"As we've been taught as guardians, we must demonstrate to the people of Egoshen by example the way we live our lives," she continued. "No matter how anyone here behaved, I've shown everyone only kindness. I never judged a person and I'm always very sincere with a joyful attitude. Because of the way I've acted and treated people, I was looked upon as an oddity. It took a very long time, but slowly a small number of people here began to trust me. In the beginning a few townspeople were curious. They'd come for a visit and we'd sit and talk. They would question me as to my attitude and behavior. My explanations were not readily accepted there was a lot of resistance."

"What happened to bring about such a change in the town?" Winston asked.

"Let me tell you the story of Carldove," Safaira smiled.

CHAPTER TWENTY-EIGHT

"Carldove was one of the very few in the town who had a lot of money," Safaira began her story, "in fact he was very, very rich, but you wouldn't know it from the way he lived or dressed. He was balding man of medium height. A little on the thin side, he had lost some weight over the past few years. The clothes he wore were drab and tattered. A rope was used as a belt to hold up his pants, which were now several sizes too large for him."

"His house looked like every other house in Calenda, small and dreary. Hidden under his bed, beneath the floorboards in his sparsely furnished bedroom was where he kept all of his money, mostly in the form of gold coins. There was no joy in this lonely miser's life."

"Chocolate was his only pleasure. Carldove would sneak off into the big city where there was an unusual and very expensive Chocolate Shoppe. Their chocolates had gold designs engraved into each piece and were filled with rich exotic flavors. It was rumored the Shoppe was owned by a wizard. Only the very rich could afford to indulge in these chocolate delicacies. People traveled from all corners of Egoshen just to buy some of these habit-forming treats. Oh yes, they were habit forming. You see the wizard put something in these chocolates, which made people crave them so they became addicted."

"The more they craved these little delicacies the more the wizard would charge them. At first a customer would just eat a few treats, but then after a short time their craving for these chocolates became strong, they would to return to the Shoppe to buy more. Their cravings intensified and their need for the chocolate increased every time they ate a piece. This forced them to keep coming back and purchasing larger orders. When they returned to make their new purchases, they found the very unusual chocolates' prices increased and continued to increase with each new order."

"Some of customers complained to the wizard that his chocolates were becoming much too expensive. Soon they would run out of money and couldn't afford these candies. The wizard laughed and told them to stop buying his special chocolates. But they couldn't stop, they were so addicted to these chocolates it became a compulsion for them acquire these delectable treats."

"Customers who had no more money left to purchase his chocolates would take the wizard aside and ask what could they do to get more of these hungered-for treats. After several days without them the addict began to feel very hungry. No matter how much food the person ate they were never satisfied, they always felt as though they were starving. Becoming so desperate, they told the wizard they'd be willing do anything he asked in order to get some of his chocolates."

"That's really all the wizard needed to hear. He began to give them tasks, stealing, robbing, cheating and a varied assortment of nasty illegal activities. Most of these people were not bad individuals, although they did have something in common. They were all very unhappy, selfish and caring only about themselves."

"Every so often one of these new criminals would get caught and be sent to prison. They tried telling the authorities about the wizard and the candies, but were laughed at. No one believed them. It seemed too outrageous."

"In prison they never lost the craving for the chocolates. Without their magic treats and unable to eat none stop, they became very agitated and very depressed. Several months without the magic chocolates, something else began to happen to them. Their complexion became pale and gray. Their skin started to wrinkle and dry, they were getting smaller and smaller. They were shriveling up and shrinking."

"A few whispers were being heard among certain customers of the Shoppe. No one wanted to believe the rumors. The idea was too frightening."

"It was the second day of the week, the day that Carldove usually went to the Chocolate Shoppe. In each hand he held a large bag of coins, which was to be used for the purchase. His mind was so absorbed in thoughts about the chocolates, he didn't realize he had made a wrong turn and was walking down a deserted alley."

"A man in a hooded navy jacket jumped out of a doorway and demanded Carldove's money. His hood was pulled down over his eyebrows and a mask covered rest of his face. Carldove insisted he was not about to give up his money. He needed it for his chocolates. The man then pulled a weapon and told Carldove he was going to take the money and use it to buy his own chocolates. The thief laughed an odd laugh, grabbed the two bags from Carldove, threw them into a larger bag and ran down the alley and out of sight."

"Carldove stood frozen unable to move, he was stunned and couldn't believe what had just happened. He walked out of the alley onto the street to look for a policeman. As he looked about, he began to think. The whispers he heard about the Chocolate Shoppe and the amazing chocolates that no one could get enough of, were they true? Were people turning into criminals in order to afford the very expensive chocolates? There was some ridiculous story he remembered hearing about a crazy man who claimed he was unable stop eating when he couldn't get his chocolates."

"Frightened and confused he decided to go straight home. He realized he didn't want to tell his story to the police about how the money for his chocolates got stolen and the circumstances of the robbery. When he returned home, he crawled into bed and curled up like a baby."

Safaira continued. "One evening I walked through what I thought was a deserted park. Coming from behind the large pine tree there were sobs. When I went to investigate, I found a man surrounded by empty food containers crying as he stuffed his mouth with food."

"It was Carldove, after offering to help him he told me to go away. He said he was beyond help; he was either going to eat himself to death or wind up losing all of his money to chocolate. Then he would be forced to become a criminal in order support his chocolate habit. If he became a criminal, he knew he'd get caught and be sent to prison where he would shrivel up and die. He was convinced that nothing "nor" no one could help him with his dilemma."

"Sitting down next to him on the ground I gently put my hands on his shoulders, gave him a warm smile, and asked him to explain what he had just said."

"He told me about the Chocolate Shoppe and the wizard who owned it. At the end of his story, I let him know in a very comforting, reassuring voice there was indeed a way to reverse his dilemma and his addiction to the chocolates. It wasn't going to be easy; it would take a lot of work and a commitment from him to transform his life, but it could be done."

"Although he didn't understand what I meant, at this point he was ready and willing to try anything. I asked him to come to my house the next evening at seven and I would begin to help him."

"With large two sacks of food hanging over his shoulders, Carldove rang the bell at my house precisely at seven."

"Sitting across from him I explained when a person is selfish and greedy it creates an opening to allow negative and destructive influences to enter into their being. By buying the chocolates continually for yourself just to satisfy your hunger and feed your habit without even a thought of possibly sharing a few pieces with someone else makes you more selfish, greedy and venerable to the magic. These particular chocolates contain magic. The magic works on greed and selfishness and therefore is able to take over your entire life. You in essence gave your power to the wizard," she elucidated he had all of this money and used only for selfish purposes. "Carldove always thought only of his wants and needs and never of anyone else. He was quite miserable. There had to be a genuine and complete change in his heart. To accomplish this, it was important to fill his life with love, joy and meaning. This necessitated him to begin thinking of others and how he could help make a difference in their lives. He needed to treat everyone with kindness and human dignity."

"Carldove asked me what I needed or what could he do for me. I told him I had no needs but there were others in this poor dilapidated town that he could help."

"The next day Carldove, still carrying his sacks of food went to see the superintendent of the two schools in Calenda and gave him money to help fix up the each of the schools, which were in great need of repair. In addition, he began a hot lunch program for all of the students."

"When he returned home that evening he sat in his chair and realized that for the first time he actually felt good about what he had done. He also noticed that his craving for food began to slightly diminish."

"By the end of the week when he returned to see me, he was able to report on a number of good deeds he'd accomplished. An idea had come to him. Perhaps he could give some of his money away to the people of the town. After all, they were very poor."

"I explained just giving money away to people was not a good idea. It may perhaps be all right at first, but after a while they'd perceive it as charity and most probably not feel good about it. It would be much better if they could somehow earn the money. There was no industry and very few jobs in Calenda. Lots of people were out of work."

"I suggested to Carldove an idea I had that might be a good beginning for everyone. Since the houses in the town were so drab and in bad condition, why not have a contest. He could give brightly colored paints to the community for the purpose of painting the houses in Calenda. The rules would be no one could paint their own house. They had to paint a neighbor's house and in turn a neighbor would paint their house. At least three bright colors had to be used on each house. Painting flowers or other designs was encouraged. A prize would be given to the house that showed the most creativity."

"The next morning Carldove began passing out flyers to all of the people in Calenda. Most were very excited about the project. The children were asked to join in and pick paint colors for the town. They picked bright and vivid colors."

"Laughter and smiles filled the air. No one in the little town could remember this ever happening before. People were beginning to feel happy. Carldove was happy as well. He lost his cravings for the chocolates and his excessive eating."

"As Calenda brightened, there was still a problem, not enough jobs. Carldove came to me and wanted to do more, perhaps start a business. He could make money and in turn offer good jobs to the people in his community. I thought it was a great idea. It was a win-win opportunity. It was sharing. But Carldove wasn't sure what kind of business to start."

"I thought for a moment as I looked around at the brightly painted house and then responded. I said the houses were so beautiful but the clothes and everything else in the town was still drab. Perhaps he could open a factory to make colorful clothes and another factory to make colorful household items. It would be a chain reaction, people could work in the factories, others would have to open shops to sell the goods. Word would spread and people from other towns could come to shop. Everyone would prosper."

"That's exactly what he did. He also began to bring some people to meet with me and told them how I helped him. He tells the story of what happened to him with the chocolates and reveals the secrets to his happiness in hopes people will understand by his example. These days many more come to learn in hopes of changing their lives."

"Carldove's transformation was so great and so many layers of illusion have been lifted from his mind that he now remembers once living in Luminatia and the wonderful life he had their before he was taken to Egoshen by Avadon. And because of that transformation he is now able to return to Luminatia but chose to stay and help others remember their lives on Luminatia."

"By sharing, Carldove has made more money than he had before and in turn has changed the lives of the people of Calenda."

CHAPTER TWENTY-NINE

"Wow! What an amazing story," Winston exclaimed.

"There are many of us here that were sent to help the people of Egoshen transform in order return to Luminatia," Safaira explained.

"Why do they have to transform in order to return to Luminatia," asked Pru.

"Because, here they're living under Avadon's illusions, they need to be able the see through those illusions before they are able to return home to Luminatia," Safaira replied. "It's fortunate you've arrived soon after Godfrey was taken. He hasn't been here long enough to have many of Avadon's layers of illusion placed on his mind. But there is something else you should be aware of, Avadon might have possibly changed Godfrey's physical appearance so you might not recognize him."

"What!" Pru exclaimed. "Then how do we know it's him if we find him? But then we don't even know where to find him. Do you know where he is Safaira and what he might look like?" Pru asked.

"No, I'm sorry I don't," Safaira replied

"Well who would know?" asked Winston.

"There are only two who would know. Avadon, who is too dangerous, unreachable and would harm you. Then there's Queen Suri, who's being held captive by Avadon somewhere in the secret castle caves," Safaira answered Winston. "There's Valeness, he's the most powerful guardian in Egoshen. He might be able to give you some assistance. But getting to him is a long, hard and very treacherous journey, even for the more experienced guardian. If you are certain you want to find Valeness, I'll take you as far as I can."

"When do we leave?" Winston promptly asked without hesitation.

"First thing in the morning, now you need to get some rest and I have to make the arrangements," she said.

"Where are we going and what kind of arrangements?" Pru asked exuberantly.

"I'll accompany you to Savell, the small fishing village on the coast where you'll board a boat to the Port of Olea," Safaira explained. "Savell is about a day's drive from here and we'll have to cross the mountains, which can be quite hazardous. The road is filled with jagged curves and it snows until mid-summer. From there the boat will take you across the Sea of Eleighten to the Port of Olea. The crossing should take about three days. This time of year, the sea is very rough and there are stories of creatures that sometimes have been rumored to attack ships. Once you get to Olea, a guide will meet you and take you on a trek inland through the jungle to Valeness' home in the Cherki Village."

Promptly at six a.m. the next morning a small tan car pulled up on the street near Safaira's house. The driver's door opened revealing a thin, frail looking older man who stepped out to open the rear door and motioned to the children to get in. Safaira stood next to the man and introduced Carldove to the children. He greeted and smiled at his young passengers, then turned to assist Safaira into the front passenger's seat.

As they made their way to highway at the far west side of Calenda, an area where very few people traveled at that hour, the early morning mist began to change to rain. At first it was a light rain but as they drove down the highway the sky turned black, the wind kicked up and it began to storm. Buckets of water seemed to be falling from the sky, lighting bolts appeared as though they were trying to pierce the roof of the small car. The strong howling winds whipped against the side blowing the vehicle all over the road and at times nearly blowing it off the road. Startling, loud, crashing thunder made the young passengers practically jump out of their seats.

Carldove mused as he slowed the car to a reduced safer speed, "Looks like some forces are trying to make our trip more difficult."

"What forces?" Pru jumped in.

"Sometimes when people are attempting to do accomplish something good, Avadon's negative forces strive to create situations to discourage them or make things more difficult. Nothing for you to concern yourself," Safaira reassured the two young passengers. "We just have to work harder and put more effort into achieving our goals."

Winston and Pru felt comforted by her answer and her confidence.

Although it felt like a lifetime, they had driven only two hours and not getting very far when the storm finally began to let up. The storm had slowed the travelers considerably. It would be another three hours before they reached the exit that would take them over the mountains to the coast. In spite of the clearing skies, there was still a great deal of flooding from the brutal storm. Driving for Carldove was still difficult.

At last they exited the highway onto the road leading them through a rural area. Along the way they noticed farm animals grazing. Traveling another fifteen miles they caught sight of the mountains up ahead. It looked ominous. Once again there were black clouds looming over the mountain, another storm was ahead.

It was about one o'clock in the afternoon, when Safaira suggested they find a spot and pull off to the side of the road to stop for lunch. Carldove removed the basket of food Safaira had packed from the back of the car. After eating and stretching their legs they all returned to the car to continue on their journey.

"The storm really slowed us down, we're about two hours behind schedule," Carldove told Safaira as he started the car.

"Don't be concerned, we'll get there when we're supposed to," she answered him calmly.

Winston and Pru admired Safaira's calm composure. It appeared whatever the challenge nothing seemed to distress her. On the drive towards the mountains the young guardian wanted to know firsthand more about Carldove's transformation. He graciously and with excitement answered all of their questions.

"There's still some significant snow in the higher elevations this time of year," Carldove announced.

"Snow, that sounds like fun, "Pru said anticipating how great it would be to perhaps build a snowman or have a snowball fight.

"Yeah! It does," echoed Winston.

"Unfortunately, we're not going to have time to make any long stops," Safaira told them.

As they approached the mountain road, a light rain began to cover the car's windshield. The deeper and the higher they traveled into the mountains the heavier the rain became and the stronger the winds started to blow. Light gusts at first, then changing into heavy gales. Chills filled the air as the temperature quickly dropped prompting Safaira to give everyone the warm jackets, gloves, scarves and hats she brought for the trip.

Carldove drove with extreme caution over the wet mountain road, which seemed to go straight up and then come straight down. The rain changed to snow flurries. Winston and Pru watched with fascination as the snowflakes fell from the sky. Pru opened the window and caught some on her hand.

Reaching the higher elevation, the powerful winds blew the intense snowfall creating large drifts, which made driving tricky. They were coming up to the most hazardous part of the mountain road where it narrowed and was filled with sharp, severe curves. In places the road was slippery and at time the car would skid. Sheer drops were visible down the side of the cliffs. Safaira sat calmly in the front seat knowing everything would be all right. Winston and Pru had not reached that level of certainty as yet they sat in the back seat white-knuckling it. They held on to the door with one hand and tightly held on to each other with their other hand.

The little car and its passengers were now driving through a blizzard. Carldove stopped the car and with Winston's help went out to place chains on the tires. These spiked chains were made especially for driving in deep snow and ice.

It took ten tense hours to drive through the blizzard and then another two hours to get down the mountain towards the road to Savell. The car got stuck several times in snowdrifts. Winston and Pru helped Carldove dig it free.

The young guardians were exhausted and fell fast asleep in the backseat. Hours later they woke in time to see the sunrise in Savell. It was a beautiful sight. A glimmer of sunshine began to peek out on the horizon. It created a luminous streak of light on the water behind the boats docked in the harbor. Fishing boats were beginning to head out on the Eleighten Sea to bring back their days catch.

CHAPTER THIRTY

The little village was quiet when they arrived. Carldove pulled the car behind a small brown and white wooden house near the water. Safaira and Carldove smiled at each other, it had been a very challenging trip. The children in the backseat were rubbing their sleep filled eyes.

The back door of the house opened and a large, red bearded man emerged to greet Safaira. She introduced her companions to Captain O'George, who invited them all into his home for a hot breakfast.

Inside in the small kitchen his wife Molly, who had been up cooking for hours, was standing near the stove. Odors of the warm bread baking in the oven and hot coffee and cocoa on the stove permeated the air. Their twenty-one-year-old son William, a tall slender young man also with red hair, walked into the kitchen and greeted their guests. "What's for breakfast," he asked with a big grin.

"That's all you ever think of is food," Molly said with a smile as she began making pancakes and introduced her son William to their guests.

As they all sat around the dining room table eating a breakfast of pancakes with maple syrup, eggs and sausages, hot cereal, and fresh baked bread, Safaira explained to Winston and Pru that Captain O'George and William were going to take them on their boat to the Port of Olea where they would meet up with their guide Oliver.

After breakfast Captain O'George and William loaded the boat with supplies for the three-day trip to the Port of Olea. Safaira stood on the dock with Winston and Pru. She made it clear to them that the Captain and William were to be trusted. They had taken Valeness back and forth across the Eleighten Sea many times and were extremely loyal to him.

A little of Safaira's confidence and certainty seemed to rub off on Winston and Pru as they said goodbye to her. They had been through and learned a lot since coming to Egoshen. They were heading into the unknown and were not afraid. Carldove came over to wish the two young travelers well. They thanked him for driving them to Savell and let him know they were very happy to have met such an amazing man.

Captain O'George asked his passengers to board the vessel. Winston and Pru crossed the plank from the dock to the deck. A loud droning sound reverberated from engine as they pulled away from land. The young passengers watched Safaira and Carldove appear to grow smaller as they sailed further out to sea. When their new friends finally disappeared from sight Winston and Pru went to their cabins to settle in below deck.

Later sitting on deck Winston and Pru reflected on their journey and how much more confident they were feeling about their rolls as guardians, but understanding there was still a great deal to learn. It had been a calm and restful day. They watched the sunset on the smooth glasslike sea for a long while until it disappeared over the horizon. It was the first time since they came to Egoshen that they felt at ease.

After a while, Pru walked to the boat's stern, she felt like being by herself. Engulfed in thought she sat watching the rippling water by the light of the full moon, wondering about Godfrey, where was he? Not only was he her brother but her best friend, remembering how they would sit and talk for hours, how they loved to go exploring. She contemplated how lucky she was to have such a great brother, even though he was almost two years older, they were very close.

When Pru was three months old, her parents disappeared. Her aunt and uncle took her in and loved her as if she were their own daughter. Godfrey was two and was thrilled having a new younger sister. He protected her, told her great adventure stories, most of them he heard from his friend Winston. Being fairly isolated in a big house in the country they were always creating their own adventures.

Stars sparkled like tiny crystals in the vast navy velvet sky. Lying on his back Winston tried to find different shapes hidden amongst the stars. He wondered how could there be so much beauty in such a negative place? The fresh sea air was exhilarating and restful at the same time. His thoughts went back to his sister, Willow and how he had been in Egoshen for almost two weeks and she does not know he is gone. He mused about the oddity of the time differences between the two worlds, thinking it may actually have been only five minutes since he left Luminatia.

It was getting late. The sea was becoming choppy and the two young passengers were about to go below for a good night sleep as they stopped first to observe the waves slapping against the ship. The movement of the sea fascinated the pair. Standing at the railing they felt the mist from the waves against their faces. After a short while the sea became extremely rough. William called for the two to come below, when Pru called out to Winston in amazement "Look! There's some sort of head in the water."

"Oh my-gosh, what is it?" he asked with alarm.

"Captain O'George, William," Pru screamed. "Come quick!"

The waves began to swell. The sea was becoming violent, as the head in the distance seemed to grow. It appeared to be part man, part octopus and part flying insect. Two fierce looking red eyes protruded from J shaped cylinders atop the hideous round human shaped head with the face of an insect. As it rose out of the sea, but still in the distance, the creature had what appeared to be human arms with long fingers resembling claws of a large flying insect, octopus like tentacles protruded from its midsection. The sound emanating from the ferocious insect like mouth was bloodcurdling.

The part of the monster that could be seen above the water now neared fifty feet in height as it began to taunt the four by brandishing its menacing gargantuan extremities in the direction of their boat. The gigantic eighty-foot arms splashed down into the water causing larger swells that hurled the boat around in the water with such force that parts of the boat began to fall apart. A substance dripped from its gruesome mouth as it snapped in their direction.

Winston, Pru, William and Captain O'George had now fastened themselves to the boat, stood paralyzed with fear as the monster continued to terrorize them. The more terror they felt the larger the creature grew, the more violent the waves became and the closer the creature came to the boat.

"Pru!" Winston shouted, "I think I've got it. I know what's happening."

"What are you talking about? Got what?" terrorized, she screamed back at him.

"Fear," he said, "Remember if you feed fear, fear will grow. I think that's what's happening here."

"Oh, wow you could be right. Yeah, the more fear we feel towards that monster, the bigger it gets. We're feeding it with fear," Pru said with a sigh of relief.

"What are you two talking about?" Captain O'George frantically asked the two guardians.

"We have to become very calm and stop being fearful. That monster feeds on fear," Winston explained. "Fear causes negativity to grow and that creature is definitely negative."

"You're both crazy," William shouted.

"No really," said Pru calmly. "Watch!"

She and Winston sat down next to each other and started to laugh, looking in the direction of the monster. "Sorry you don't scare us you big ugly thing," Pru said smirking and sticking her tongue out at the monster.

The monster flailed and shrieked as Winston and Pru sat calmly taunting it with smiles and laughter.

William shouted, "Look it's not coming closer, it's going away from us and, and," he stuttered, "And it's actually getting smaller."

Realizing the creature was shrinking and maybe his young passengers were on to something Captain O'George said, "William, it's looks like it's gonna be ok son."

Now seated on the deck the four grinned, waved and laughed in the direction of the once ominous monster. The swells began to get smaller as did the creature until it finally faded out of sight and the sea was as smooth as glass.

The boat had sustained a lot of damage but with some patching it would make the remaining two-day trip to the Port of Olea.

The patched-up boat arrived four hours behind schedule. William recognized Oliver standing on the dock and waved to him.

CHAPTER THIRTY-ONE

"Looks like you've had a rough crossing," Oliver said with some concern in his voice.

"You don't know the half of it," William replied with a grin on his face, as he tossed the rope to secure the boat to the dock.

"Are your passengers ok?" Oliver asked trying not to appear alarmed.

"Ok, no they're amazing," William, said pointing to Winston and Pru who had just come up on deck.

"Hi! I'm Oliver your guide, heard you had a tough crossing.

As the youngsters disembarked from the boat Pru said whimsically, "Oh! Nothing we couldn't handle."

"We'll have a bit of breakfast first and then we'll begin our journey to Cherki," advised Oliver. "Everything's ready to go."

"They have one heck of a story to tell you over breakfast," William told Oliver.

The Port of Olea appeared to be somewhat primitive in comparison to some of the other places they have seen in Egoshen.

Two donkeys ready to pull an old-fashioned wagon filled with supplies waited near the boat.

"Is that for us?" Pru asked astonished at the rugged mode of transportation.

"It's the best and safest way to get through the jungle. We have to stay off the main road. Too dangerous." Oliver told them.

Captain O'George and William had to attend to repairing their boat, so they said their goodbyes as Winston and Pru climb aboard the wagon. One donkey pulled as the other packed with more supplies was tied to the back of the wagon.

"There's an inn a short distance away where we'll stop to eat," Oliver told them.

Oliver a tall man with an imposing stature, a stocky build, bright blue eyes and a reassuring smile stood at six foot four inches. His grey frizzy hair and sun wrinkled face made his age to be perhaps in his mid-fifties.

The village of Olea was small with a few unpainted simple rustic wooden structures. The roads were unpaved and dusty, the weather hot and humid. Children ran barefoot in the streets.

Oliver let them know he is aware of their ability to transform and suggested it would be safer for them to become an old man and an old woman for the journey through the jungle. He explained they needed to stay off the main roads because the jungle was filled with treacherous creatures that prey on people who travel on those roads. They are especially partial to children.

After breakfast Pru and Winston, per Oliver's request transformed themselves into an elderly couple as they climb back aboard their rustic manner of transportation. They flanked Oliver as he drove the donkey drawn wagon towards the jungle.

"Can you tell us about Valeness and how do you know him?" Pru questioned Oliver not knowing much about the great sage.

"It's a long story, but I guess we have a lot of time," Oliver answered as he began to relate the story.

CHAPTER THIRTY-TWO

They listened as he told them of the first time, he first met Valeness twenty-two years ago. Oliver, at the time was a pirate on the much-feared ship called The Delivida. They would sail the seas looking for ships that carried wealthy people and cargo.

It was midnight. Oliver was the lookout, when he spotted a ship in the distance. Through his telescope he was able to read the ships name, The Three Doves. He had heard of that ship and it was rumored to carry very valuable cargo and rich passengers.

The captain of The Delivida was a cruel, ugly pirate by the name of Grawgo. He was a short wiry man with two black front teeth and a huge scar running from his ear to the corner of his mouth. Grawgo took great pleasure in stealing, frightening and hurting people.

Oliver sent word to Grawgo that the ship The Three Doves was ahead. The Delivida sailed quietly, without lights until they were close enough to board the unsuspecting ship. The passengers and crew were all asleep. The lookout on The Three Doves who was supposed to be awake had fallen asleep while on duty.

This night The Three Doves had a very rich cargo. The Baron of Chidrick was traveling to the city of Briette with trunks filled with gold, diamonds, rubies and emeralds to be given as gift to Nelvenda, the young woman he planned to ask to be his wife. An entourage of seven traveled with him to guard the treasures.

Also traveling on The Three Doves were ten additional passengers. There were two wealthy middle-aged sisters, an elderly couple, a young mother with her six-year-old son accompanied by his new puppy Max, a young man of twenty, a couple on their honeymoon and Valeness. Other than the passengers there were twelve members of the crew including the captain and the young man sleeping on watch.

Very quietly The Delivida sailed close to The Three Doves. When the two ships were nearly touching, twenty-one of the meanest, nastiest pirates silently crept aboard the passenger ship. Grawgo, using just hand gestures directed this ornery band of brigands to their positions. Upon his signal they rousted the passengers and crew and bringing them all on deck. Oliver's job was to make sure that the crewmember sleeping on watch did not make any noise before the signal.

A gunshot rang out. That was the signal. Pirates standing ready outside the cabins with weapons drawn kicked in the doors. Passenger and crewmembers were startled and frightened awake. They panicked as the pirates dragged them up on deck. Sounds of screams, crying and shouting filled the air.

Dressed in their nightclothes, the captives stood shaking on deck. Grawgo sent eight of his men off to pillage the ship, while the rest stayed with him. Great pleasure was taken in terrorizing people. It gave the pirates a feeling of power to have such control over their victims. In fact, these hooligans were really very weak, frightened, miserable thugs.

Oliver continued with the tale. Valeness looked Grawgo in the eye and said, "Please take what you want but leave these people alone."

"Please ya say," Grawgo cackled, "Ya be their savior, ah," he taunted as he grabbed Valeness by the arm and dragged him to the railing. "Gimmie that little pup the kid is hanging on to," he ordered me, and I immediately tore the puppy from the young boy's arms and handed it to Grawgo.

As the boy started to scream and ran towards Max, his mother grabbed him and held him tightly.

"Ok savior, you gotta a name?" he said as he looked smugly into Valeness' face.

"Valeness," he answered in a calm voice.

"Here's the deal," Grawgo growled as he put the puppy in Valeness' hands. "You toss the pup over the side or um gonna toss ya over the side." he said haughtily.

Unruffled, Valeness took the puppy and walked over to the boy, touched his shoulder. The boy immediately calmed down as Valeness handed him Max. Looking Grawgo in the eye Valeness serenely said, "Do with me what you want, but I won't kill anything, even if it means my life."

Infuriated at what he perceived was Valeness' arrogance. Grawgo ordered Fondell and Oliver to bring Valeness to him. As they were about to grab hold of him, Valeness put a hand on each of their shoulders. A tingling feeling went through their bodies. He looked into their eyes and smiled. Fondell and Oliver stopped stunned in our tracks, suddenly not wanting to harm him. Grawgo, angered at the lack of obedience of the two pirates, ordered two more pirates to bring Valeness to him. Once again Valeness put his hand on each of their shoulders and the scenario repeated itself, two more pirates stood before him stunned in their tracks.

Grawgo not understanding what had happened ordered two more pirates to fetch Valeness and once again the same thing happened. The remainder of the pirates looked on in total fear. Oliver stood straight and turned to Grawgo and the rest of the pirates with an odd look on his face then confidently and authoritatively told them to drop their guns and return to their ship immediately. Fondell and a group pirates stood behind Oliver in support of him.

Frightened and bewildered all but Grawgo obeyed, returning to their ship. Grawgo stood with his mouth hanging open thinking how could this have happened, defeated by a man with no weapons.

Valeness walked over to Grawgo, put his hand on his shoulder, smiled, looked him in the eye and said benevolently, "I'll see you soon."

Grawgo returned to The Delivida. Oliver, Fondell and four of the pirates remained with Valeness. The passengers returned to their cabins and the voyage safely continued to its destination.

At the end of Oliver's chronicle Pru said, "Wow, he can change people's minds just by touching them." In an exuberant youthful voice, coming out of the mouth of what appeared to be a seventy-year old woman, "Valeness sounds amazing I can't wait to meet him."

CHAPTER THIRTY-THREE

After nearly five hours of traveling through the hot and very humid jungle, Oliver pulled on the reins and stopped the donkey. "We need to let the donkeys a rest for a while," he said as he climbed down off the wagon, unhitched one donkey and unloaded the packs off the other donkey. He then secured their leads to a tree.

Oliver took Winston and Pru to a heavily shaded area about thirty feet away across a clearing next to the stream. There they could rest, eat and he would be able to keep an eye on the donkeys. He told them it would be safe while they were here to transform back to themselves. It was a welcome relief. Staying in character as the old couple was beginning to drain their energy.

Oliver reminded them to stay alert, although this spot appeared peaceful and safe, danger could crop up at any moment. The jungle was abounding with sounds of birds, animals, insects and other creatures. As they sat under the tree near the stream, they saw bugs everywhere. There were some very strange large, brown with green striped gooey caterpillars, huge grey beetles with three heads that made an eerie clicking sound.

Pru wanted to go wading in the stream, but Oliver told her that the stream has eryxthizoms. Which are large snake like creatures covered with razor sharp needles that emit a poisonous substance. When this substance is released from the needles it paralyzes its victim. Once paralyzed it crushes its victim then eats its prey.

"That's gorily comforting," Winston remarked.

"What's that?" Pru asked sounding a little alarmed at the sudden ear-piercing screeching sound coming from the distance.

"Get in the water," Oliver shouted at his two companions.

"What!" Pru anxiously replied, "But the snakes."

"Get in the water now," he insisted.

Coming towards them rapidly, traversing the clearing was a hideous odd-looking creature resembling a huge ball of spiders about nine feet across with sixty-four hairy legs protruding out in every direction. Despite the fact that it was one creature, it appeared as if eight gigantic spiders had been connected at their heads.

Fine silk strands began coming from this enormous creature. Winston and Pru jumped into the stream while Oliver drew a huge machete from his belt in an attempt to fight this creature. In a matter of seconds, it was too late the creature wrapped Oliver in a web like cocoon. He was unable to move.

The spider like creature, a multarach, stood at the edge of the stream hissing and screeching at Winston and Pru. A clear sticky substance oozed from its mouth. To the two young guardians it appeared as if the creature was drooling. It was not coming in the water. That was why Oliver wanted them in the water. He knew it would not follow them. But downstream swimming towards them were two eryxthizoms.

Winston screamed at Pru, "Grow, Pru grow fast and as big as you can. He grabbed hold of Pru and focused every part of his being into transforming his body into a huge giant. Nothing was happening, he could feel the fear building. There was no time to be afraid. His consciousness had to change now, if they were killed on Egoshen it would be all over. They would never return to Luminatia. Then it happened his body shot up forty feet into the air. Suddenly, he had to let go of Pru, she too began to grow and when her feet hit the water with a big splash, she crushed the two snakes. The ball spider began to hurl sticky silk strands at them. It did not seem to care how large they were. The creature wanted to capture them in its web.

They were using all of their abilities to try to remain large. The two were not accustomed using this magnitude of energy and it took a tremendous degree of power and concentration to maintain their size.

They were running out of time. Oliver was in trouble and they had to do something fast if they were going to be able help him. "Help me pull this tree out of the ground, we'll whack that thing with it," Winston instructed Pru, pointing to a twenty-foot tree on the other side of the stream.

Pru and Winston tugged and shook the tree until they pride it loose from the ground. The tree was much heavier than they thought. The two of them had to work together in order to lift it up in the air and swing it at the multarach. But before the tree could hit that gargantuan creature, the spider launched its sticky strands with such intense speed creating a huge web of protection for itself.

When that did not work, the pair attempted to throw boulders, but with no success. "Water," Pru said. "It won't come into the water and a web can't protect it from water."

They manifested large leaves as carrying vessels, filled them with water and began to toss the water at the spider, once again nothing. It had no effect on it. "What else, what else?" Winston thought out loud as he tapped the palm of his hand against his forehead and forcing himself to stay in control.

"Fire! Let's try fire," Pru shouted to Winston. "Look, there are a couple of dead trees over there.

Winston struggled to maintain his forty-foot body as he grabbed both trees and Pru quickly gathered some of the dried leaves surrounding the trees. "We need to start a fire; I don't have any matches, do you?" breathing heavily he called out to Pru.

"No, we need to think," she responded vehemently. "There's got to be a way to make a fire. I know we can do it. We just have to. It's too humid to rub sticks together that won't work."

"I've got it, I've got it," Winston shouted excitedly at Pru. "Our medallions, we can use our medallions to start a fire."

"How?" she asked.

"We need to make a pile of dead leaves and brush. The medallions are a very shinny gold. I'll hold mine at an angle towards the sun and you hold yours at an angle down towards the dead leaves. If we keep both medallions close enough and at the right angle to each other, we'll get a reflection and enough heat to start a fire."

The multarach continued to taunt them from near the water's edge hissing, screeching and continuing to hurl its silk strands in the direction of Winston and Pru. They put the leaves and brush on one of the large boulders in the stream. Once the leaves ignited, they each took one of the dead trees, soaked one end it in the water to prevent the entire tree from burning, and then put the dry end into the fire.

With both trees ignited they very quickly proceed towards the creature. At first the silk strands began to disintegrate as the multarach attempted to create a thicker web of protection for itself but that too caught fire.

"Pru, at the count of three, throw it like a spear," Winston instructed his friend. "One, two, three." The trees soared through the air, bull's-eye, they hit their target. As the multarach went up in flames Winston and Pru return to their normal size.

"Quick, we need to help Oliver," Pru said alarmed as they both race towards their fallen guide covered in a very sticky cocoon.

Removing the multarach's casing from Oliver was proving difficult. Pru tried to pull away the covering from his mouth, but her hand stuck to the mass of silken threads and she was unable to pull it away from his face. "Whatever you do, don't use you other hand," Winston ordered. "I'm gonna go to the wagon, there's gotta be something there we can use to free you." He ran to the wagon and frantically began search the supplies, pulling things out of bags and boxes when he found a knife and a bottle of oil. "I think this will do it," he said trying to sound hopeful.

Hurrying back, he knelt beside Oliver. Opening the bottle of oil, he poured some on the knife. He took a leaf and covered it too with oil as well as his left hand. The oil prevented the leaf and his hand from sticking to the cocoon. Placing the leaf on Oliver's face, Winston felt for his mouth and very carefully with the oiled knife made a slit in the casing allowing Oliver to get more air. He repeated the procedure near Oliver's nose.

With her hand still stuck to the cocoon, Winston poured a small amount of oil on the skin of her hand and cautiously began to peel the sticky substance off, finally freeing Pru. "There's not a lot of oil left," Winston said as he used the remainder of the oil to uncover Oliver's face.

"We've gotta somehow get him into the wagon He's so huge," said Winston looking concerned at Oliver laying there unconscious, his breathing shallow and knowing that he and Pru were all alone in the jungle.

"Winston, we were just forty feet high a little while ago. We pulled trees out of the ground like they were weeds. All we have to do is grow again and put him in the wagon. That should be easy. What's your problem?" she asked him exasperated.

"Don't you think I know that? I've been trying to change back but nothing's happening. I have a feeling that I used so much energy staying forty feet for so long, it's just not working," he replied.

"Ok then, I'll do it," she insisted as she began to focus her energy to transform, but nothing happened. "What are we going to do, I can't transform either," she said frantically.

"Pru, look over there," he said pointing to the banana tree a short distance away. "There are some huge leaves on that tree. I can climb up and cut some leaves and we can wrap them around Oliver so we won't stick to him when we touch him."

Winston ran to the wagon to search for something to cut the leaves. In a large leather pouch under the seat he found a small axe, which he immediately put into his belt.

"Please be careful," Pru cautioned Winston as he began to climb the twenty-foot tree.

"Just hold on tight, i can do it," he told himself, his heart pounding as he grabbed the next branch and carefully took the axe from his belt and slowly began to chop away at the thick banana leaf until it fell to the ground. Breathing rapidly, he climbed a little higher and cut another leaf.

"I think one more will do it," pru shouted up to winston as she eyeballed the size of the leaves against oliver's body.

"Ok," he said as he cut the last leaf and climbed down.

"Pru you put the first leaf on oliver's upper body starting just under his chin, i'll put another one on his lower body and then we need to carefully roll him over one his stomach so that we can wrap the rest of the leaves around his back," he instructed as the two began to wrap oliver, wrapping the third banana leaf around his legs.

"How are we going to get him into the wagon?" Pru asked looking towards the carriage of the wagon, which was about four feet from the ground. "He's too heavy for us to lift and i don't know when we're going to be able to transform again and we can't just leave him here."

"I know," he said sitting on the ground with his eyes closed and his hands coupling his face trying to rack his brain for some solution.

"Winston, i'm scared, what are we gonna do?" She asked sitting down next to him.

"Maybe, if we could get some branches that are strong enough to hold his weight and put them together to make a slant board, we lean it up against the wagon and pull him on," he thought aloud.

"Do you think it could work?" She asked.

"I don't know! I don't know what else to do," he said sounding frustrated. "We've gotta try something, we just can't sit here."

"Ok! I'm ready," she said getting up trying to glean some enthusiasm. "What size branches do we need?"

He looked around until he found a branch, he thought might be strong enough for the job. "Here about this size should do it. Pru we've gotta be really careful, keep your eyes open, we don't know what's out here in the jungle." He warned her as they both began to gather the branches nearby and then had to venture a little further from their base to collect more.

Winston bent down to pick up another branch when suddenly there was loud gurgling roaring sound. Then an ear-piercing scream, it was pru.

"Winston, help…no, no," then silence.

He could barely breath it was as if his heart had stopped, in shock he froze for a second never had he felt such terror, not even on the ship when they saw the monstrous creature. His mind numbed with the thought something might have happened to pru. Dropping the branches, he raced through the jungle towards where he has last seen her, tripping over fallen branches, brush and tree roots protruding from the jungle floor. Thorns from brush tore at his skin. He did not feel a thing. It took him only minutes to get back. His heart racing, his body shaking and his face and arms dripping with blood as he reached the wagon. There was no pru in sight. He turned to where they had left oliver laying on the ground wrapped in banana leaves. He too was gone.

Over heated, trembling and panting with tears running down his cheeks, winston ran off in all directions looking and calling pru's name. All he heard were just the sounds of the jungle. He searched and shouted her name for hours. The sun had disappeared and was replaced by darkness. Totally drain he returned to the wagon and fell to the ground in despair.

"Please! I need help," winston sobbed pleading with the two donkeys tied to the tree. "I hope you guys can find your way home," he said in a quivering voice as he untied them. With great effort he climbed on to the back of the larger donkey and held the reins of the other. He kicked his heels into the donkey's rump and the animal lurched forward quickly, causing winston to drop the reins attached to the second donkey.

The donkey appeared to know where he was going as the second donkey followed close behind. His energy totally depleted; winston wrapped his arms tightly around the donkey's neck. They traveled for hours in the darkened jungle. Winston was hot and thirsty, in his haste he forgot to bring the jug of water. Never in his life had he felt such desperation, so helpless and hopeless as he did at this time. The brief preparation he had as a guardian as well and the positive guidance and reinforcement he had received all of his life growing up never prepared him for the overwhelming feeling of hopelessness he was now experiencing. First, it was the loss of his friend godfrey. Pru was so certain that if they came of egoshen, they would be able to get him back. He felt her certainty she was always so optimistic it was contagious. But now she was missing, would he ever see her again? "What did we get ourselves into? We didn't have enough experience. We just weren't ready for this. We were so in over our heads. Oh, pru where are you," he continued to sob until he was so exhausted he could barely hold on to the donkey.

He could not find it within himself to see or feel that everything would be all right. He just clung to the donkey, as his brain seemed to deaden. His throat was parched, he was dizzy, his arms and legs were tingling and then nothing. It was as if his brain fell into a deep dark abyss.

CHAPTER THIRTY-FOUR

"Hello young man," Winston heard a voice off in the distance. Everything was black. His eyes were closed and he had no awareness of his surroundings. He attempted to open them, but his lids were so heavy they would not move. Slowly he forced them to open. There was some light, but everything was surrounded in a fog. He saw the figure of what appeared to be a man in the fog. "You are all right Winston," he heard the voice proclaim, "you were dehydrated and exhausted. You have been unconscious, but you are fine now. Take it slow, you are still a little disoriented."

"Where am I? Who are you?" Winston insisted as the haze in his brain began to clear. He gazed into the soothing eyes of the old man standing next to him.

"Sit up slowly, Winston," the man with the grayish brown beard and wire glasses said gently. "I am Valeness, you are safe. This is my home."

"I've lost her. It's all my fault I shouldn't have left her alone. She screamed, she called for help and I ran to find her. I couldn't find her, she's gone," Winston rambled on and began to sob. Valeness took the young guardian's hand and held it. Winston was not acting or feeling much like a guardian at the moment. His demeanor was more of a frightened young boy. A soothing warm energy flowed from Valeness' hand into Winston's body as a feeling of calmness came over him. "Pru, I couldn't find her. I felt completely helpless and hopeless."

"You were experiencing Avadon's negative forces. Your powers as a guardian were not strong enough yet to fight them off. You became a victim of the environment he created. It is what happens in Egoshen to people living under the control of Avadon. When something seems hopeless, that is when our work begins. Nothing is ever hopeless. We need to have conviction that we will be shown the way," Valeness explained.

"I was told you know everything about what happens here. Do you know what happened to Pru? Is she ok? Where is she?" Winston asked.

"She has not been harmed. She was taken by harufanks to Avadon's caves," Valeness replied.

"What about Oliver?" the young boy asked.

"He has been taken there as well," the elder guardian stated.

"He was wrapped in a cocoon from a huge, hideous spider like creature. How do we get them out of there?" Winston anxiously questioned.

"First, you have to get you strength back and work on your conviction, without both you'll never succeed."

"I'm ready now," Winston insisted enthusiastically.

"No, you are not. The reason you were not able to transform when you needed to was you allowed your energy to become depleted and negativity entered your consciousness.

"I'm rested, I feel strong," he reassured Valeness.

"I am not referring to your physical energy. It is the energy in you mind, your thoughts. There is no room for even the slightest doubt if you have any hope to succeed. Any uncertainty or shred of fear will deplete the positive energy I am talking about. It will inhibit your ability to use your powers. Should you need to transform and should you be successful in transforming for a time you might not be able to maintain that form. We have the ability and the tools to perform what others might consider miracles. Your medallion it one of those tools, the inscription in the emerald is a great source of strength. You must meditate on it and it will help you to get the answers you seek," Valeness counseled.

"You have only been a guardian for a very brief time and were not fully prepared for the journey you took upon yourself. Your intentions were admirable and you have done fairly well with your creative thinking and transformations. I know you have good potential but there is much you still need to learn. What you want to do is extremely difficult even for an exceptionally experienced guardian and if you are not properly prepared you will indeed fail," Valeness affirmed.

"How do I know when I'm properly prepared?" Winston questioned.

"We never know ahead of time if we are properly prepared. All we can do is our very best and have great certainty, faith and trust in the positive energy force within us. Valeness continued with his teaching.

"So how do you have great certainty if you can fail?" Winston asked.

"First of all, what is failing? Failing is a preconceived notion that *you* know how an outcome should be. If it does not turn out the way *you* expect or want the outcome to turn out, *you* believe you have failed. That is not true. Having great certainty means knowing a situation will happen the way it is meant to happen or it needs to happen. We might not understand the reason why but that is where trust and faith come in," he answered.

"Let me give you a simple example," Valeness continued. "A man having great certainty and faith knew he wanted to buy a gift his friend would enjoy. Knowing his friend liked candy; he thought a raspberry candy would make a good gift. Doing his best to find this candy, the man went to store after store and no one had this particular candy. Unhappy and feeling he had failed, the man had to settle for a chocolate candy. He gave the chocolate candy to his friend. His friend thanked him and confided to him that he had received several boxes of raspberry candies and recently he discovered he had become allergic to raspberries. The friend was grateful for the chocolate candy."

Accepting and understanding Valeness' answer Winston continued with his questions, "How is it you know about everything that is happening in Egoshen?"

"There are a great number of entities from the Kingdom of Lights here in Egoshen who are not in physical bodies. They travel about and keep me informed as to what is happening," the great teacher responded.

"Is Pru ok? What about Oliver is he all right?" Winston asked with great concern.

"At this time, yes," Valeness said.

"What happened to them? Where are they and how can we get them back?" Winston persisted with his questions.

"As I said earlier, they were captured by Avadon's harufanks and were taken to the Castle in the Caverns. Rescuing them will be extremely difficult and nearly impossible. The place where they are being held is very dangerous," Valeness informed Winston. "Avadon spends a great deal of time there and it's over run by treacherous creatures."

"I don't care how dangerous it is I've got to get Pru out of there and bring her home. It's my fault she got captured, I've gotta get her out," Winston lamented.

"First, it is not your fault. Had you been there they would have taken you as well," Valeness explained.

"Can't you go get them?" Winston pleaded. "You're a powerful guardian."

"Winston there is so much more you need to understand about Avadon. First, we have to use our powers with great care. The Order of the Light was formed after Avadon left Luminatia therefore he is unaware of our existence. It is paramount in helping all the people in Egoshen for Avadon to be kept in the dark about guardian. Should he become aware of our existence, he would know we have been sent here to assist his people in returning to Luminatia and that would be catastrophic. He would wreak havoc on the people of Egoshen. Whatever difficulties they are suffering now would intensify vastly by Avadon's retaliation should he feel his powers were being usurped," Valeness explained to Winston.

"What would he do to hurt people?" Winston questioned.

"Over the centuries Avadon has become a sadist and is a master of illusion and pain. He can create anything, any horrific circumstance to make people's suffering immeasurable, from a plague, to war or other ghastly acts. His evil is boundless, especially when provoked, he takes great pleasure in seeing people in pain."

Valeness continued, "We are cautioned before we come to Egoshen to never allow ourselves to come into close proximity of Avadon. Beings from the Kingdom of Lights continually inform guardians as to Avadon's whereabouts so we may keep a safe distance. Guardians have energies which people of Egoshen lack. Avadon has the ability to sense our energy but at this point he is not cognizant of the fact we are guardians. Unfortunately given enough time and exposure to us he might come to realize who we are and our purpose. If somehow, he does come into contact with one of us, we are forbidden to use our powers as a guardian to protect ourselves. We must appear, as just an accidental wanderer from Luminatia and the consequences could be grave. That person would be tortured in some way, loose their powers and possibly be put to death. As guardians we must be prepared to sacrifice our lives to prevent our identities from being revealed and to protect the people of Egoshen. My energy as a guardian is so strong, I would be discovered by Avadon immediately and therefore would be of no help to you or your friends."

"Then what am I going to do? How can I get Pru and Oliver back?" he was determined and insistent to press on to rescue his friends despite these new obstacles.

"Winston you must understand, you would be risking everything including your life. There is almost no chance for you to succeed. This would be incredibly dangerous," Valeness warned.

"It doesn't matter, I have to try. Valeness, I will try," Winston insisted emphatically.

"Then proceed in a stealth like manner, but you, young man, do not have the experience or the knowledge necessary for this undertaking. You have had very little training as a guardian prior your arrival in Egoshen. Although this could be a small advantage for you since you are still a child and your energy as a guardian might not yet be strong enough for Avadon to perceive you as a threat. You have learned a little about transformations but you are only able to sustain that state for a short time. You have barely touched on the use of medallions. One of the functions of the medallion here in Egoshen is to meditate and connect with Queen Suri and beings from the Kingdom of Lights. We are able to get messages from them. You have been hearing what seems like voices in your head because some of those beings have attempted to assist you, but without proper instruction in its use the assistance has been limited," he patiently explained.

"Can you teach me what I need to know? Please, I have to try to help Pru," he said resolutely.

"Do you have to help her because you are feeling guilty about what happened to her?" Valeness asked.

"No, she's my friend. I love her. I need to do everything in my power to get her back. I used to think of her as my best friend Godfrey's little sister, she could be a pest and sometimes she would make us laugh, but Pru always wanted to help. She's got a big heart. And since we've come to Egoshen, well Pru's had more guardian training then me, she always tried to help and encourage me. I'm going to help her get home," he adamantly insisted.

"Yes, I understand," Valeness replied with compassion. "You have heard this many times before. What you must always be conscious of as long as you are in Egoshen is the enormous negative energy. It is very heavy unlike the energy in Luminatia. Even though you are a guardian, it still has strong influences over you. Not to the degree is affects Avadon's subjects. Understand as guardians we might have certain powers but we also have limits, unlike King Shadel we are not immortal."

"You will be greatly challenged. Your training will offer you some protection from Avadon's negative control. He will be un-yielding in his attempt to play with your mind. Constantly be aware of what you are thinking. Should something negative enter into your thoughts, it is imperative for you to immediately see it for what it is, just one of Avadon's tools to distract you from your goal."

"My young friend, we have all been given various gifts, abilities and talents. We must learn to use them properly if we are to overcome obstacles. For example, Winston, you have not been able to conquer your fears and doubts," Valeness explained.

"When I transform, I don't feel afraid," Winston averred.

"You are unaware but the fears and doubts are there. For instance, when you transform for an extended period, you might feel fatigued and unaware that some doubts are beginning to permeate your subconscious mind. Random thoughts may catch you off guard like 'I'm feeling tired. Keeping this up is hard. I'm not sure I can keep this transformation up.' They are fleeting but harmful thoughts, therefore be aware of what they are, but do not give into them to them. That what Avadon's counting on," Valeness counseled.

"Then how do I stop these thoughts from creeping into my subconscious? If it's the subconscious, you're not aware they're there," Winston asked feeling puzzled with Valeness' explanation.

"Good question," Valeness continued. "When you are accomplishing a familiar task as a guardian, your intentions are good but a bit of doubt flows in you. Or you are prevented from performing a task. It is because those pesky pessimistic thoughts and feelings are present. Transforming necessitates a great deal of energy and concentration as does utilizing our other powers. Normally we don't pay attention to our random thoughts, which leaves an opening for doubts. As a guardian, you must be aware of your thoughts at all times. It is hard to do but with practice and focus it can be achieved."

"Also, you require complete certainty in the positive energy force in order overcome those destructive beliefs and insecurities. You must recognize and believe in your power as a guardian. Only with that degree of certainty will you have the ability to resist the negative energy force and perform your mission as a guardian. Once that is accomplished, we are able to achieve amazing things," Valeness explained to Winston.

"Then when I transform and it's necessary for me to stay transformed if I start to get tired or need to use other powers, all I have to do is remember what you've just taught me and I should be ok," Winston asked amazed at seeming simplicity of the lesson.

"Yes, it may sound simple," Valeness said sensing Winston's thoughts, "but it is also quite difficult. We have a great deal of preparation if you are to undertake this journey."

Curious, Winston asked, "Valeness where does the positive energy force come from in Egoshen?"

Valeness smiled, "From Queen Suri. That is the reason she allowed herself to be kidnapped, to help infuse her positive energy force into us. At present it would be constructive for you to be in a quiet place and reflect on our conversation." Valeness suggested the waterfall a short distance from the camp. The setting there was tranquil and picturesque.

Winston walked there in virtually a trance like state, overwhelmed by possibilities and what he still needed to learn. He sat in this peaceful environment with his eyes closed for hours. The hypnotizing sound of the waterfall allowed him to go deep within his mind while removing the outside world from his consciousness, as he tried to grasp all that had been revealed so far.

Later Winston sat with Valeness for what felt like an eternity, taking in everything his scholarly mentor taught him at lightening speed. It was as though he was absorbing the information straight from Valeness' mind. In reality it was not an eternity Valeness had stopped time.

"How do I get Pru and Oliver back safely?" Winston asked with a new air of confidence.

"The Chaga's will help you. Their species were here long before Avadon. When he arrived, he destroyed most of their race. The ones who survived have a great aversion towards him. I have helped them and they trust me. They can be dangerous and want to be left alone. But they are also the only ones who know where to find the entrance to the Castle in the Caverns,'" Valeness explained.

"How do I find them?" Winston asked.

"The donkey will take you to their habitat. Then they will find you," his mentor told him.

A short, wiry man with two black front teeth and a scar from his ear to the corner of his mouth brought the donkey to Valeness.

"Thank you Grawgo," Valeness said.

"Grawgo!" Winston exclaimed startled into utter amazement. "Grawgo the pirate?"

"The very same," Valeness smiled. "He tends the animals and is very good with them."

"Name's Jakey," Grawgo said handing Winston the donkey's reins. "He's a smart one. A might stubborn, but he'll take good care of ya."

"Thank you," Winston smiled.

"Remember all that you have learned. Take great care, the path you have chosen will be fraught with danger. Keep in mind everything is not as it appears. Your certainty is sure to be tested. Negativity is strongest in the Castle in the Caverns," Valeness said as he bid his young student off on his journey.

CHAPTER THIRTY-FIVE

The sun beat down on Winston as he climbed on Jakey's back. The jungle felt so hot and the air so humid, it was hard to breath. As he rode off, he glanced back to see Valeness and Grawgo waving to him. His head filled with Valeness' words. Everything seemed so simple yet profound. The rhythmic sounds of the jungle accompanied Winston as he cautiously watched the lush green ferns and the trees covered in vines, some with vibrant flowers that lined the path. He savored his time with Valeness, a kind, gentle man with such great wisdom. The anticipation of what lied ahead played in Winston's stomach like a swarm of dancing butterflies.

New instruments joined the jungle's music. It was the sound of children coming from the distance. "What are children doing out here?" Winston wondered as he continued riding on Jakey's back. He felt something hit him behind his right ear. Looking around he saw nothing. "Hum, I guess something must have fallen off a tree," he thought as another object propelled into his chest. Startled he looked about again and could not see where these flying objects were coming from. When out from behind the trees stepped about a dozen or so young filthy looking children with long tangled, dirty hair wearing nothing but what appeared to be leaves woven together. In their hands were slingshots. They each had a pouch tied around their waists filled with berries, which they continued to launch at Winston. They could not have been more than five or six years old. The children did not seem to speak, they just grunted, making a series of indistinct sounds and pointing.

"Are you Chaga?" he asked as they continued to pelt him with berries. They did not seem to understand a word he said. They flanked his left and his right. Then they began to giggle like little children playing a game. "Chaga?" he repeated.

Another dozen or so children slowly came from behind trees up ahead. These were older, about Winston's age. Something was not feeling right. The children had stopped giggling and began humming an eerie rhythmic beat as they marched on either side of Winston and Jakey.

"This is getting creepy," he thought as some of the children began making odd faces at him, taunting him. He was suddenly able to see what these children actually looked like. They were not the illusion of the cute dirty scamps his eyes had just seen. These children were ugly and distorted with long arms and claw like fingers. They had elongated noses with large black circles around their deep-set grey eyes. There were large sharp jagged teeth protruding from their mouths. The skin on their faces appeared as if it was melting.

Suddenly he was finding it difficult to breath. These children were sucking the air from him when he heard Valeness' voice in his head "use your medallion." Winston slowly put his hand on his neck and slid it down under his shirt until it touched his medallion.

"These are the Salva, Avadon's castaway children," the voices of the beings from the Kingdom of Lights warned him. "You must protect yourself by using the wind. Once normal children, Avadon has taken these youngsters from their parents and experimented on them by casting spells and using potions. They never pass the age of twelve and remain that age forever. Avadon has transformed them into dangerous creatures who will only continue to grow more evil."

Barely able to breath, Winston focused on the meditation following Valeness' instructions. He watched as the wind began to stir up from the calm air of the jungle. It blew in a circle around Winston and the donkey, acting as a barrier between them and the children. The wind forced the children away from Winston. Relentless, they tried clawing at the air to reach him but the strong wind's circle became wider and wider until the children unable to get to Winston were pushed back off the road.

CHAPTER THIRTY-SIX

As he headed towards the Chagas, he thought in amazement how in a relatively short time with Valeness' instructions how much he had learned. Life as he knew it before on Luminatia would never be the same again. He had changed. Once he was an ordinary young boy who loved adventure stories, flying his malgrid and hanging out with his friends. Would he ever be able to go back to that life? No adventure story he had ever read or imagined could compare with what was happening in his life now. No longer a boy. Yet not a man, what was he? Winston was not quite sure exactly where he fit.

What he did know was he was a guardian with a lot to learn, he was at the threshold of more life changing experiences. He felt strong. He felt certain. He felt confident. He felt something slimy crawling up his leg. "What!" he said aloud as he looked down at his leg and watched as a large fat worm made its way up his leg onto Jakey's neck. "Gross!" he said as the worm transformed itself into a duplicate Winston.

"You not that great to look at either," said Winston's mirror image.

Stunned and startled, Winston blurted, "What? Who? Who are you?"

His mirror image, still dripping with slim announced, "I Chaga. I called Ob. Who you?"

"I'm Winston. I'm so glad to have found you. Valeness sent me. I've come to get your help. Avadon's kidnapped my two friends and took them to the Castle in the Caverns. I need to get them out. Please will you help me?" Winston begged.

"Ob can't say," his slimy mirror image told Winston. "You have to ask others. I take you to others but animal must stay here. He be safe, he go back home to Valeness," he said as he returned to his worm form and slid back down Winston's leg to the ground.

Winston left Jakey under a tree in the shade and followed Ob into the jungle away from the road until they came to a clearing filled with mounds of dirt. Ob tapped his tail several time on the ground. Hundreds of worms emerged from the mounds of dirt, taking one look at Winston, they all transformed into more mirror images of the young guardian. Winston rubbed his eyes in disbelief of the sight of hundreds of mirror images of himself. "Hello, I'm Winston," he said, greeting the sea of Winstons seated on the mounds before him.

An image close to him replied, "Winston, I Nav, leader of Chaga. Ob say you need help to rescue your friends from Avadon evil castle."

"Yes, will you help me, Valeness sent me?" he asked watching as the slim dripped from his replicas.

"Valeness," he echoed looking around at the Chaga who all seemed to be nodding in approval. "If Valeness sent you, we help. His energy good, you energy good too. You can transform, yes? Nav asked.

"Yes."

"You must change to Chaga. We leave when light of sun goes away. You must travel between Ob and Nav we keep you safe. First it necessary for you to now transform to Chaga and learn to dig in ground." Nav instructed Winston.

The thought of becoming a slimy worm and crawling into the ground made Winston feel queasy and slightly repulsed, feelings he dares not reveal to his hosts.

The slim served to keep a worm's body cool in the jungle, Winston observed about his transformation to Chaga. He had been practicing at being a worm for several hours. Winston had to learn something of the Chaga's methods of communicating.

A series of tapping and telepathy, he learned enough to be able to know what to do when they would travel to the castle.

"Time come, Winston. You prepared?" Nav asked the fat worm slithering next to him.

"Yeah, I'm ready," he answered, still a little uncomfortable with his new body and noticing the hundreds of brown slimy worms that had gathered behind Nav.

"We travel in group of three. You stay between Ob and Nav," Nav instructed Winston the worm. "There be few groups in front of us, many groups traveling behind us. We arrive at castle before sunrise. Whatever happen, you must not transform back to original Winston body, understood?" Nav firmly ordered. "To get you to castle safely you must listen to Nav. When Nav say dig deep, fast, you obey," the leader instructed the novice worm as he directed the Chaga into position.

Winston slithered in his new form in between Ob and Nav as they headed towards the Castle in the Caverns. He tried to imagine what Pru would say if she saw him traveling with the pack of worms. She did not like worms. They grossed her out, she said they made her skin crawl. He laughed to himself for a moment at the thought of Pru's expression when she saw worm Winston and friends. He knew she had to be ok but wondered what she had endured. Traveling as a worm seemed a little slow for Winston. He contemplated transforming back to his own form and getting there faster, but remembered Nav's warning and he continued to slither.

From his vantage on the ground, everything seemed enormous. Plants that he might have stepped on as a young boy seemed gigantic. Proportionately the plant seemed more like the size of a tree in Winston's present state.

Nav and Ob stopped short as the ground beneath them began to tremble. "Stop, Winston," Nav ordered telepathically.

Winston halted, "What's happening, why is the ground shaking?" he asked in the same method.

"It harufanks, get to trees, to bushes, to vines, hide," Nav frantically warned the Chaga telepathically then turned to Winston in the same mode, "Winston, follow Nav up tree, quickly."

Winston obeyed and followed Nav's path up the nearest tree Ob was close behind. They slithered up the tree until they were about eight feet off the ground, and then Winston saw them, the lime green beasts. The harufanks. There were about twenty of them coming down the path. Some revealed stump like protrusions resembling arms and legs. There were those that slithered along the ground and some that hobbled along on their stumps. The eerie ear-piercing sounds emanating from these beasts sent chills down Winston's spine.

When he and Pru left Luminatia, there were three of these hideous creatures, but seeing twenty at one time was incomprehensibly beyond horrific.

Nav and the Chagas waited in hiding until they were sure the harufanks were far enough away and they were safe. "Harufanks like to eat Chagas and snakes," Nav explained. "Sometime after Manfreed von Neever arrive in Egoshen, he sent harufanks to Chaga's mounds. It was big city. They try wipe us out. New ruler did not like Chaga. Valeness fill many wagons with boxes of wet sand for Chaga to travel and brought Chaga safe to jungle." Sensing they were safe he said to Winston, "Ok to travel again."

They reached the sight of the foot of the mountain, which hides the Castles in the Caverns, just before sunrise. "This far as Nav can take friend Winston," Nav explained to Winston as they said their goodbyes. "Winston must stay Chaga until safe in castle. Entrance behind three small mountains."

CHAPTER THIRTY-SEVEN

Slithering along the cracks between the wall and the floor of the cave, Winston spotted a number of flying bats and decides staying above ground could be dangerous. He burrowed down about a foot underground and traveled deeper into the caves. Traveling nearly several hundred yards, Winston attempted to check the surface again. Poking out of the ground with caution he looked about, he was alone.

Pushing his worm body through to the surface he was stunned when suddenly he felt something grab him. He found himself in the claws of a birdlike creature that was now flying up near the roof of the cave and heading into a tunnel. It happened so fast he did not have time to transform back to himself. The tunnel was bustling with activity. It was too risky to transform and too risky to stay in his present state. Winston had been warned he was not to be seen in a transformational state while at the Castle. Should Avadon or one of his special visionary emissaries observe him in a transformed state, they possessed the ability to see through that transformation to the real Winston. That would put the young guardian in grave danger.

The birdlike creature arrived at what seemed to be a nest with two baby birds. "Oh no! I'm gonna be dinner for these birds, Whoa! Winston think quick!" he exclaimed trying to remain to remain focused. "I'm in a nest and no one can see me other than these birds, I've gotta chance it," he thought as he transformed and added razor sharp needles protruding from every part of his worm body just as the mother bird was about to feed him to her baby birds. The birds could not touch him he was safe for now.

He peered over the side of the nest hoping the tunnel would clear out, but how would he get out of the nest. The nest was about thirty feet from the ground. With the razor-sharp needles in his worm body he could not slither down the wall and if he got rid of the needles, the bird would get him again.

It was several hours later when the tunnel finally emptied. "I've got it," he laughed to himself. Checking to make sure everything was clear, Winston the worm made his way to the edge of the nest then quickly transformed into a soft ball and rolled out of the nest to an easy landing on the ground. He immediately returned to being Winston.

There were unnerving noises in the distance, it sounded like screams, remembering Valeness' words he remained calm.

Carefully making his way through the tunnel he heard the whimpering sounds of a child quietly sobbing. Unable to see anything, he continued walking along close to the wall. It was then he saw the boy huddled in a small curve in the tunnel wall. There was something familiar about him. "Arnie," Winston said startled and surprised. "Arnie is that you?" he asked the boy he and Pru had met when she was nearly hit by a car.

"Ya, who are you?" the boy asked.

"It's me, Winston, Pru and I met you a few days ago," he said kneeling down next to the boy, still not sure he could be trusted. "What happened to you? Why are you here? How did you get here?"

"I remember you, the magician, but you told me your names were Will and Jill," Arnie said looking at Winston suspiciously.

"Oh yeah!" Winston had to think fast. "Those are the names we use when we're being magicians. How did you get here?" Winston repeated, attempting to quickly change the subject.

Arnie accepted Winston's answer and explained to him how he wound up in the Castle in the Caverns. "I snuck out of the house in the middle of the night I couldn't sleep. I had a fight with my little brother Pauly after dinner and my mother took his side. She always takes his side. He's her favorite. I was really mad at Pauly so I took his favorite hat and tossed it the neighbor's trash. I decided to go the playground and swinging on the swings for a while. I've gone to the playground before in the middle of the night and I've always been ok. This time an older kid was there and he started talking to me. All of a sudden, he turned into this ugly monster and the next thing I remember was I was taken to this awful place called the Cave of Screams. There were lots more of these ugly monsters. They're called the harufanks and there were other hideous creatures there too. Lots of people there were screaming. They were being tortured I was so scared. The harufanks were holding the people while King Manfreed did something terrible to them. There was like an energy force coming from them and going into the Ruler. He was smiling and the people were in pain, it looked like he was sucking their energy. He was enjoying watching these people suffer."

"How did you get away?" Winston asked.

"They were holding me near the entrance to the cave when one of the other harufanks needed help from the one that was holding me. He let me go and probably thought I'd be too scared to move. But I ran out of there as fast as I could and then got lost. I wandered around for a long time and couldn't find the way out," Arnie said as he began to sob again. "Why are you here, Winston?"

Winston explained to Arnie that he was there to rescue Pru and Oliver.

"You've gotta be crazy, Winston, we've gotta get out of here. It's really dangerous," Arnie warned.

"I can't leave until I find Pru and Oliver," Winston insisted.

As the two boys searched the caves, Arnie whispered, "Winston I thought I heard a girl's voice coming from inside this door."

Winston slowly opened the door. Arnie pushed him into the room and slammed the door shut. "What! Why did you do that?" he demanded.

Arnie eerily smiled at Winston and then using a very devious, authoritative voice gave him an order. "Watch!" Right before Winston's eyes Arnie changed. He was no longer a young boy; he had transformed into a tall thin woman.

"Hello Winston," she said with a condescending smirk on her face. "Oh! You think you're ever so clever but I've tricked you, haven't I? I'm not your little friend Arnie. There is no Arnie. I'm Queen Feendra, the sister to your King, Manfreed von Neever," she announced sarcastically feeling quite proud of her trickery. Years of living with Avadon as Manfreed in the destructive environment of Egoshen had a damaging affect on the once arrogant and selfish sister of King Shadel. She became vicious, cruel, bizarre and irrational.

"You claim to be a magician, an illusionist yet. However, you are just a pretender who is only able to use tricks to create the illusion of transformations, but I am the one with the real power to actually transform," she bragged not realizing Winston was a guardian and his ability was as real as hers. His steadfast demeanor infuriated her. He should have been fearful and impressed by her importance and acted according.

"There are others here who once thought they were so great and believed they were better than us, more powerful than us, more beloved than us. Ha! Ha! Ha!" she scoffed as she ranted and rambled. "We are the ones who are powerful and our people love us and if they don't… King Manfreed will make sure they do." Angeen brashly sneered.

"Who could you possibly have here that was so powerful and great?" Feigning naïveté while knowing all the while she was referring to Queen Suri, Winston provoked her into revealing the name of their prisoner.

"Well we have Queen Suri here, she thought she was the great queen and had such power, but here she's nothing, just a sad retched old creature," Feendra snickered. "If we can make her into nothing, what do you think we are able to do to a smug little magician like to you?"

"I don't believe you," he baited her defiantly. "You're lying, if she's here I'll bet she still has all her powers. Show me, prove to me that she no longer has any of her powers."

"You silly insolent little boy, you don't believe me, well I'll show you that pathetic hag," she bragged as she grabbed his arm pulling him through the tunnels down to the deepest level of the caves where the Queen was imprisoned. Opening the door to her dungeon she pointed, "Look, you see little boy, there is the once great Queen. I told you she is nothing but an old hag, see for yourself," she laughed as she pulled him back and locked the door. "Now there's a dungeon waiting for you right down this way," Feendra pointed as she pushed Winston through a nearby door, closed it and turned the lock. "I'm going to have you brought before King Manfreed tomorrow morning. Oh! He is going to enjoy draining your brain," she boasted. Her behavior was ghoulish.

His time and training with Valeness were paying off, he felt nothing but sheer determination and confidence. Winston waited for a while until he was sure Feendra would not return. Then transforming himself into Chaga he once again burrowed into the ground and slithered towards Queen Suri's cell. Once there he became Winston.

Queen Suri looked at the young guardian, "you're very brave and clever Winston."

"Thank you, Queen Suri. You know my name?" Winston shyly replied. For the first time he looked into the eyes of the Queen, although she appeared old and frail and was dressed in a tattered drab robe, her exquisite emerald green eyes expressed her great strength.

"Of course, I do. The reason I appear this way is an illusion I've created for Avadon and Angeen so they will believe I'm weak and pay me no mind," she expressed. "This is the real me," she smiled as she transformed for a brief moment into the Queen Winston remembered seeing in Myadora's vision.

"Wow!" Winston was speechless. "But I thought we're not supposed to transform because Avadon can see through our transformations," he asked.

"My power is so much greater than Avadon's, that he is unable to see the real me," she explained. "Therefore, I'm able to use my positive energy force without being detected."

"I know why you're here. It's to rescue Pru and Oliver," she informed him.

"And Godfrey too," he reminded her. "Can you please help me?"

"I can tell you where they're being held, it's the fourth door to the right outside of the Caves of Screams. You must discern how to rescue them yourself or it won't work. Pru is very weak and frightened. Her guardian powers cannot be utilized. Remember under no circumstances can you use your powers as a guardian in front of Avadon. This quest will be extremely dangerous and you might not succeed. It's necessary for you to go deep within yourself to find the answer. Draw on my positive energy force for strength. But now you must return to your dungeon. Someone will be coming in here soon to check on me and they shouldn't find you here. Winston, I'm proud of you, you're very brave. Continue to stay strong and remember Valeness' words or you might lose everything as well."

CHAPTER THIRTY-EIGHT

Once again Winston became Chaga and slithered back to where Feendra had imprisoned him. He did not sleep at all. Instead he spent the entire night meditating on an answer. At daybreak, he heard the sound of a key in the lock. As the door to his dungeon opened, he saw a big burley man dressed in a black robe, a white apron with what appeared to be bloodstains was worn over the robe. Behind him outside the dungeon was a harufank. The man grabbed hold of Winston's arm and led him down a tunnel to a long staircase. The harufank was now in front leading the way up the stairs. Horrific blood curdling screams could now be heard. Winston assumed they were entering the Cave of Screams.

Following the harufank, the burley man continued to drag Winston until they arrived at two large wooden doors. The harufank pushed open the doors and shoved Winston inside the dismal looking room

Seated in the middle of the room on an ornate throne chair was a tall good-looking man who Winston immediately recognized. It was Avadon. Remembering the warning not to look into Avadon's eyes, Winston instantly stared past Avadon.

"And who exactly are you Winston? Avadon asked sounding particularly pompous, "and what are you doing here?"

"I need to find my friends and get them out of here," he replied not sure of what to say as Avadon attempted to case a spell on him.

"Oh, you do, do you. That's rather ambitious and presumptuous of you and how do you expect to accomplish such a task? Avadon quipped at the audacity of this boy. "Do you know who I am?" he asked defiantly. Avadon was now puzzled, as the spell he attempted to cast was not working on Winston.

"No sir, I don't," Winston lied trying to sound dim witted.

"I'm King Manfreed von Neever," Avadon announced. "You're the magician, Feendra told me about. I don't believe you're from Egoshen now are you? You must be from Luminatia but how did you get here?

Not wanting to disclose information about guardians, "My friend and I found a window in the forest and decided to investigate. We were curious and we turned up here," he said all wide eyed and innocence.

"Magician, what kind of magic do you do?" Avadon asked.

"At home I do magic tricks for children, I can pull coins out of their ears," Winston responded hoping to sound believable.

"Boy! Look me in the eye," Avadon ordered.

"No Sir I can't!" Winston insisted.

"No!" Avadon roared. "Who do you think you are to say NO to me?"

"I'm sorry, Sir," Winston began to lie again, putting on a most naïve performance. "But there was a time when a man asked me to look into his eyes and, without my knowledge, he hypnotized me and made me do bad things. So now I never look into anyone's eyes."

Seeing he was not creating fear in this apparent naïve boy, Avadon annoyed decided to try another tactic. "Bring this boy's friends to me," he ordered the harufank. "Let's see what this wretched young insolent creature does when he sees what will happen to his friends. He will never again refuse to comply with my orders."

In a short time two harufanks deposited Pru and Oliver into the room. "Winston," Pru looking weak and hopeless moaned as she recognized her friend. "Oh no they've got you too."

"Oliver and you two pathetic children," Avadon sarcastically taunted, "I'm going to take great pleasure in watching you suffer. Fear is such a rush Winston and for your friends I intend to create some magnificently gruesome experiences. I know you'll enjoy watching."

"I'm taking you to the Cave of Screams now. It's a place that stimulates my imagination. I find screams of pain such an inspiration," he proclaimed with a devilish smirk on his face.

He grabbed Winston by the arm pulling him towards the cave, while the harufanks followed carrying Pru and Oliver. As they entered the cave Avadon gloating, said, "I think you should have a tour of the wonderful spectacles going on here at present.

"Here in Egoshen we have such a marvelous array of interesting creatures that work so well in the Cave of Screams. I just have to decide which creature will do the best job in each situation. And there are so many situations. Here for instance are the alum worms doing their job and doing it so well," the sadistic ruler said pointing to a man hanging upside down.

A glass tank containing hundreds of two-headed alum worms with sharp fangs on each head had been placed beneath the man. His hands were tied to the bottom of the tank. These creatures were crawling up his arms to his body. As they traveled upwards, they dug their fangs, which discharged a red-hot burning substance, into his flesh. The man was screaming in agony.

Winston winced in revulsion, unable to believe the unbearable horror he was witnessing.

"Here's a favorite of mine," Avadon said as they passed a man strapped to a table. There were tiny gray spherical beasts with a very thin half-inch long spike protruding from their heads. They crawled to the man's hands and feet and slowly jabbed their spikes under his finger and toenails. While little red insects covered his body sucking bits of his blood as they injected him with venom creating an unendurable itching sensation. Writhing in excruciating pain and extreme discomfort, he screeched profanities.

"Here's one I'm particularly proud of," Avadon smiled at Winston as he directed the boy's eyes towards a pit filled with very thin ribbon snakes. A woman tied down in the pit sat screaming hysterically. Her mouth was held open by a steel device called a mouth gag. Every so often a snake slithered up her body reaching her mouth. When it entered her mouth, she would gag as it slid down her throat to her stomach and into her intestines. Her body became horribly distended. Outlines of snakes moving about under her skin were visible on her lower body.

"It's now your friends turn," Avadon said giving the order to shackle the two frightened captives to the wall as he held onto Winston. "Let the entertainment begin," Avadon sneered.

"Please, sir let me take Pru's place," Winston shouted after seeing the kinds of torture this monster was capable of inflicting on his victims.

"Aren't you the brave young boy? No! Of course not," Avadon grinned ghoulishly. "I want you to watch and see how imaginative I can be. First, I'm going to have their bodies covered with a special mud that will harden like a rock. It's really the closest thing to being buried alive, wonderfully claustrophobic. The bottom of their feet will be exposed, as will their mouths. The satea's will have easy access through their feet and we leave the space open near their mouths, we can hear their screams so much better that way. We can also see their mouths foaming."

Winston watched in absolute horror as two harufanks began to encase his shackled friends in mud. Pru pleaded for help while Oliver shouted profanities at Avadon. The mud hardened instantly.

"Now for the gripping climax to this event. It's a slow process, we don't want it to end too soon," Avadon announced in a disgustingly gleeful manner. "The satea will enter through their feet. These splendid insects will crawl up under their skin into their bodies releasing gloriously agonizing toxins through their sharp stingers. These toxins will eat part of their skin away. Your friends' screams will be like music. Have you ever heard a symphony of screams, Winston? It's magnificent."

Eight hideously deformed children entered the Cave of Screams each carrying a box. Winston recognized them as Salva, the evil children he had encountered on his way to the Chaga.

"Winston, do you like my young friends? You and Pru will become one of them when we are finished here," Avadon gloated. "That's if Pru survives."

Addressing the Salva, Avadon said, "Now my young lovelies you have gifts for Pru and Oliver. Open your boxes and let your friends out. They have work to do."

The Salva children placed the boxes on the ground and removed the lids. The boxes were filled with tiny satea bugs. Each bug with sharp stingers protruding from their mouths and claw like pinchers waving from their double tails were released.

"There's a substance in that dried mud that attracts them. Watch!" Avadon reveled.

Winston stared horrified as a few of the insects found their way to bottom of Pru and Oliver's feet and began to pierce their skin with the pinchers in their tails.

"Ow! Help me Winston please," Pru cried out in panic as she began to sob. "It hurts a lot."

Winston tormented by seeing his friends tortured and in such great pain not knowing what else to do, closed his eyes and focused on drawing into Queen Suri's energy force. Then taking a deep breath, he turned to Avadon and steadfastly declared, "Sir, I will make a bargain with you."

Startled and intrigued by Winston's audacity Avadon laughed, "And you a child, what could you possibly have to bargain with?"

"If you will agree to release Pru, Oliver and Godfrey and allow them to safely return to Luminatia immediately and unharmed. I am willing to allow you to inflict the same pain equal to the all of the pain you have already inflicted on the people of Egoshen on me and any further punishment you desire I will accept," Winston with great conviction in his voice, calmly stated.

"What!" Avadon shrieked knowing that part of the agreement he made with Shadel was if anyone agreed to take on the same pain of the people of Egoshen, Avadon must not harm them. He must release them and grant them a wish. Avadon will then immediately loose his control and evil powers over that person. Only Avadon and Shadel knew of this term in the agreement. "Who are you?" enraged, the sadistic ruler roared.

"I'm just a simple boy from Luminatia who got lost in this place," Winston said in a courageous, calm and quiet voice, unaware of the agreement between Avadon and Shadel. "I want to make sure my friends safely get home."

Avadon realized if he did not adhere to their agreement, Shadel with his powers would know immediately and would remove Avadon's immortality. Once that happened, Avadon would cease to exist. He would be dead.

Once Winston offered the ultimate, to take the same pain that was inflicted on all the people, Avadon had no choice but to grant his wish and freedom. Winston immediately found himself back at the window entrance to the tunnel on Luminatia, which brought them to Egoshen. Next to him stunned and sitting on the ground was Pru and Oliver.

"What happened? Pru asked looking around puzzled.

"I'll tell you later," he said feeling despondent that they had to leave without finding Godfrey.

"But what about Godfrey?" Pru asked, still shaken from her ordeal, "We left him behind."

"What about me?" Oliver asked as he slowly transformed back into Godfrey. "I'm here, why would you leave without me?" he said feeling completely disoriented.

"Godfrey!" Pru and Winston shouted in unison. As they realized Avadon must have transformed Godfrey, who loved pretending to be a pirate, into Oliver when he was taken to Egoshen.

Winston and Pru brought Godfrey home and put him to bed. The next morning when he woke Godfrey related to Pru a very strange dream he had about how he was a pirate named Oliver. He told her in this dream she and Winston came to rescue him in some very strange place.

She laughed and said, "Godfrey that sounds like such a crazy dream, I don't think I'd repeat it to anyone, they'd think you nuts."

"Pru, I'm not sure I want to play the part of a pirate in our adventures anymore," Godfrey said sheepishly.

"If you only knew," Pru said silently to herself.

The two young guardians planned to explain how they found Godfrey wandering in the forest with no memory. After all they could never tell anyone what really happened and reveal their true identities.

CPSIA information can be obtained
at www.ICGtesting.com
Printed in the USA
LVHW010631150720
660481LV00004B/125

9 781913 359843